• • •ON THE MOVE

· · · ON THE MOVE

Harriet May Savitz

The John Day Company · New York

An Intext Publisher

Library of Congress Cataloging in Publication Data

Savitz, Harriet May.
  On the move.

  SUMMARY: After becoming involved with other handicapped youth, a formerly shel-
tered paraplegic girl realizes she can also learn to lead an independent life.
    [1. Physically handicapped—Fiction]   I. Title.
PZ7.S26640n   [Fic]   72–12093
ISBN 0–381–99641–7

The John Day Company, 257 Park Avenue South, New York, N.Y. 10010

Published on the same day in Canada by Longman Canada Limited.
Printed in the United States of America
Designed by The Etheredges

Second Impression

···**ON THE MOVE**

· · · CHAPTER 1

He sat off to the side of the basketball court, his tall lean body taut in the wheelchair, his face showing no trace of emotion as he gazed up at the clock in the back of the gym. Ten more minutes and the game would be over. The wheelchairs on the court continued to race back and forth as the basketball shot into the loop time after time. Skip rubbed the arms of his wheelchair. The game was close, a two-point difference all the way. It was more than competition in this game. It was hatred, a bloodbath. Each time the two teams had played, there had been a battle at some point on the court. Underneath the shots and fouls, behind the tight playing and the skill, seethed an unsettled battle, and Skip wondered whether it would be settled tonight.

"Hey, Skip, it's close."

Bennie's face broke into a smile as he came off the court. The sweat poured down his back and his arm muscles, full and breaking with veins from his endless hours in the wheelchair, now flexed, then relaxed.

"Go ahead, Skip. Take care of them."

Skip nodded and rolled into the game. He knew the team depended on him for defense, for getting the ball to the guy who could drop it in. For the last year, ever since he had joined up with the Zippers, he had been the center of the wheelchair basketball team.

He was needed, yet no one really knew him. He was depended on by four other players, yet he was a stranger to all of them. "He's tough," they'd say sometimes in the locker room. "Skip has four layers."

Skip wheeled over to the center of the court, rubbing his shoulders. His fingers, raw and bleeding from the other wheelchairs that had tried to block him, felt the thud of the ball as it was passed to him. He held on tightly and looked around. Two bounces and a roll on the wheels . . . he moved slowly . . . bouncing twice, maneuvering his wheelchair back and forth around in a circle, feeling the smack of steel as the other wheelchairs tried to block his way, looking for the opening. Over to the side, he saw Mac with his hand held high, his red hair shining like a lantern.

"It's yours," Skip yelled and passed the ball over the reaching hands that tried to block his view.

The sound of leather could be heard around the gym and the crowd went wild as the ball flew into the net. The score was tied again.

Buddy put his arm around Skip's neck. They had nicknamed Buddy "Drop-out" affectionately, for as a class-one paraplegic, his balance was off. Four times at least during every game, Buddy would drop out of his chair and roll onto the floor. The audience would grow hushed, awed, frightened at what happened. But Buddy was a ham. He could handle it. "You've got to give the crowd something," he'd say. "They paid for some excitement."

So now, wheeling next to Skip, he smiled. "Should I drop out," he asked, "for entertainment time?"

"Come on." Skip didn't smile back. "We're going to beat the hide off them."

"Just keep cool," Buddy cautioned. He knew Skip's temper. He knew the fire inside that could be ignited by the wrong word, or by a stray look. But they needed Skip. He could pass a ball like a thunderbolt clear across the gym. Buddy had caught some of those balls. Sometimes he felt his chest would cave in from the impact.

Buddy understood Skip. When he himself had been crushed inside that automobile ten years before, the anger had come like a growing cancer inside the pit of his stomach. But Skip was young yet, and the mine that had blown his leg to bits only two years before left the anger in him, fresh and untamed.

"Watch Bob. He's got a setup."

Skip wheeled over to the edge of the court. His hands bothered him. He had forgotten to cut his nails and the wheels had caught him too many times already.

He watched his team move man to man, trying for the opening. Bob edged over to Buddy and called his name. Buddy lost his balance and the chair tipped forward. Someone from the opposite team grabbed the back of his chair and tilted him upright. The whistle blew.

Time out. The Green called it. Skip looked over toward his coach, Glen Harris. Both teams wheeled off the court.

Glen huddled the team together, a white towel hanging limply over his shoulders. As coach of the Zippers, he knew each man on his team well, and he knew how to reach him.

"Keep them out," he said. "We've got to break the tie. Keep them busy, out of the scoring zone. Skip, keep it cool." He put his hand on Skip's shoulder.

They all remembered the last time they had played the Boston Greens. Skip and Joe Kelly had fought over a jump ball, and then it was team against team, with paras rolling on the floor and wheelchairs tipping over until the game was called off. They had promised themselves it wouldn't happen again. Joe Kelly had kept his distance tonight, because the called-off game had hurt both teams. But no one had forgotten. The League competition was close this year, each of the competitors needing every win. None of the teams was in for sure as a winner. A canceled game, especially because of a fight, would hurt everyone.

Bennie Blue came back into the game and replaced Jim Christy. Bennie's enthusiasm caught on as he hit each of his teammates gently on the hand as he came by their wheelchairs.

"We're gonna kill them," he said. Bennie was just

nineteen. He had been stabbed in the back during the
week the baseball scouts were observing him at his high
school. During the long nights since, he remembered
clearly how they had come up to him that week and said,
"Bennie, you're good. When you graduate, we have a
place for you in our organization." And then came that
sick, silent night, when, lying on a stretcher with sixteen
years of living behind him, he had thought it was all over
for him. Often he had talked with Skip, telling him how
he thought he would never hear the shouts and hoots,
even the boos of the fans again. That knife wound in the
dark alley of his neighborhood had cut away more than
his ability to walk. It had taken him away from the baseball field, from what he thought would be his whole life.

"Wake up, Bennie." It was Skip's voice. The ball
shot like a well-aimed bullet into the pit of Bennie's
stomach. But he smiled. It brought him back to the whis-
tles of the fans as he heard some of them call out his
name.

"Throw it in, Bennie."

"Break the tie."

"You can do it."

The shouts rang out clear, almost clearer than when
he had been standing on the mound with his classmates
cheering him on from the stands. His hands were sweaty
but he held on tightly, despite the jabs at the basketball,
despite the other wheelchairs crowding around him. His
long fingers, supple from hours of guitar playing, now
played a tune of their own as they controlled the ball,
guiding it around the spinning wheels, spinning it this
way and that, taunting, teasing, then withdrawing it back
into his lap.

"Throw it in," someone called from the stands.

Bennie looked over toward Buddy. He was caught between two wheelchairs, blocked off. Skip was moving like a gust of wind, trying to get near the basket, but Kelly was shadowing him.

Skip looked back over his shoulder. His face was red, his eyes angry. Obviously Kelly was mumbling something to him, trying to cut into the cool control that Skip was working at.

Bennie took a deep breath. "Here goes, lady," he said, and his long arms shot up.

Swoosh. He just barely heard it. The crowd was standing shouting his name and it took a moment for him to realize he had broken the tie, bringing the Zippers out ahead.

"Holy cat . . . holy cat." He shook his head and laughed. A whistle blew.

Skip was on the floor, his hand clutching at his knee. The referees went over to help him into the chair. He pushed them away, and backed his way into the wheelchair, his black hair almost as dark as his eyes. Kelly had tipped his chair. It was no accident.

Buddy rolled over with Mac and Bennie behind him. They glanced over quickly to the stands, where Glen stood, a worried look on his face. Even the crowd seemed to sense that the breaking of the tie was the least of what was happening on the court.

The next three minutes of the game ticked by slowly. Joe Kelly kept on Skip's tail, constantly knocking his chair just within the rules. The score was 60 to 58, and Skip could sense a victory. He moved cautiously, trying to keep the scoring players out of the key, backing them up off the court, looking for an opening to grab the ball. He had been shoved deliberately. He could tell by the look in Kelly's eyes that his spill had been planned, but the referees hadn't caught it. He bit his lip, and remembered biting his lip when the doctor had said, "The leg's got to go, Skip. Infection has set in."

With it, Skip remembered the mine blowing up, somewhere on a patch of land called Vietnam . . . the blood spilling across the fields as they carried him to the ambulance, the last rites of the priest as he lay in the hospital emergency ward wondering why he felt nothing but thirst, wondering why he didn't feel as though he were dying at all.

He learned about death that day, that day only a couple of months after his seventeenth birthday. Death came in little spurts. It came when they operated and operated and operated again, each time taking more of his leg, until it all was gone, the right leg, and where it was, was nothing. He had bitten his lip when he looked down that day and nothing was between him and the floor on the right side where a foot should have been. The emptiness on the bed, where something should have been, filled the room with a scream and he knew it was his, a cry that sounded more like the wail of a dog, but it was his cry . . . his last cry.

For then control had set in. This was it. No one would know or hear that cry again. The layers built in Skip, month after month of covering up, blanket over blanket of self-control, until the cry inside was stifled; and though it echoed through him during the night, it never was heard again.

Now, feeling Joe Kelly's breath hot behind him, he

reached for that control. Just one minute, he kept saying to himself, hold off for one minute.

But then he looked up and he saw one of Kelly's teammates look toward Kelly and the ball shot across the gym. Bob, one of the best pick men on the Zipper's team, tried to intercept but failed. Kelly reached out, Skip reached too in a desperate attempt to block the ball and maintain the lead in the game. The ball hit his hands, then fell.

Kelly rushed for it. He bent down over the wheelchair, and grappled for the bouncing ball but Skip was after him, and both their hands fought for possession.

The wheelchair bounced the ball from Kelly's hands and Skip had it. He yanked it into his lap and turned his wheelchair around. But Kelly was behind him. Just as he reached out to stretch his arms in front of Skip's face, the whistle blew, ending the game.

Kelly's arm went down on Skip's arm. The audience stood up. The whistle blew again, but neither player heard it. Skip tried to pull away his arm, but Kelly held on.

"You amputees don't belong in the game. Play with the walkers," Kelly sneered.

The scream inside Skip moved around now, the control weakened as the words taunted him. With the wooden leg supporting him, he could forget about the time he had to take it off. He could forget how he wanted to smash the leg against something, the way his dreams had been smashed, the way he wanted to smash Kelly's face right now.

Skip whirled his wheelchair around, breaking Kelly's hold. Then swiftly, before Bennie could stop him, he put his strong arms around Kelly's throat and hung on tight, catching him in a hammerlock that turned Kelly's face red.

There was no control now. Just wild anger. Anger at emptiness. Anger at frustration. Anger at his inability to cope with wooden legs and mirrors that showed no reflection where a leg should be, anger at people who said, "You're lucky you have the other leg," and, "It could have been worse." What was worse than living with a limp and cold something called a foot that had no warm blood running through it? So he hung on to Kelly's neck while the wheelchairs swarmed around them.

The coach and referees were caught between the wheelchairs, and though arms pulled at Skip's strong muscles, he still would not release his grip.

Through his half-closed eyes, Skip could see the shocked faces of the audience, their mouths agape, hands to their faces, and then one face . . . a girl with hair like silver gold hanging long around her shoulders and tears running down her cheeks. Her hands were clutched in her lap. Someone was standing next to her, talking to her but she wasn't listening.

Skip let go. Kelly coughed and gasped, and someone was shaking Skip, asking him what happened.

Skip turned away from the silver gold hair. He took the ball from his lap and slammed it against the wall with all the strength remaining in his hands. Then he sat, facing the wall . . . alone.

· · · CHAPTER 2

"Mom, you should have seen them. What an exciting game." Sandy's long blond hair swished back and forth as she took the dishes carefully out of the cupboard.

"Dad and I will really have to make it our business to see one of these games."

"Carrie should come too." Sandy rested the dishes on the sink and reached for the napkins. Her blue eyes squinted, searching the dark pantry closet. "We're out of napkins," she said.

"Honey, put it on the shopping list."

Sandy added napkins to the long list on the chalk board hanging low on the wall by the telephone. The telephone and the chalk board and many other things in the house were put in places within Carrie's reach.

"You know, they practice in our high school gym every Friday night." Sandy took the silverware out of the drawer. "It's funny, but no one I knew ever even went to watch them practice. I mean, there they were, the whole team, all along, right in our own school."

Carrie wheeled in, her lap filled with a sewing basket and some clothes. The table was about level with the wheelchair and Carrie stretched slightly to put her sewing basket on the edge of the table.

"Will I be in the way while you're setting the table?" Carrie asked.

Sandy shook her head no. "I'll work around you." Sandy put on an apron and brought the dishes over to the table. "Will you come to the next game with me? You'd really love it, Carrie." Although her sister was twenty-one, four years older than Sandy, her delicate features and bangs that cut gently across her forehead made her look much younger.

Sandy watched the auburn hair shake as Carrie answered, "No, I'm really not interested in sports."

"You would be if you saw it." Sandy would not give up. Ever since her sister had been taken ill with polio, ever since that fateful day thirteen years ago, when, "Mommy, I can't move my legs," had echoed through the halls and caused fear to hang on every word, Sandy had been her older sister's support, her other legs. Whenever possible, she would take her outside, bring her places, try to share with her. Although Carrie was unable to go to school and had to have a special tutor, Sandy tried to bring in the school atmosphere as much as possible. There were many class parties at the Dennis home. Sandy's friends were encouraged to come and go with the freedom of the rest of the family, and Carrie was there to share in the laughter. Through the years, she had taken to sewing and lately had been doing mending to bring in some income.

Whatever Carrie couldn't get outside, Sandy and her parents tried to bring into the house. It was a good family, a warm one, with loving and caring deeply etched in each of their faces. Sandy, now a senior in high school, a cheerleader, tall and lanky with freckles dotting her nose, worried about Carrie lately. Whereas before, when company came, Carrie's wheelchair promptly appeared, now she spent more and more time down in the basement with her sewing machine and the mending. "I'm tired right now," or "I'll be up later," was the usual answer that came drifting up the stairs to Sandy and her guests. The smiles, and Carrie's cheerful good morning, were less and less familiar. And the braces. That had bothered Sandy most of all. Carrie had always walked a little each day, using her braces. It was difficult for her, especially with the tenderness she had developed under her arms from the crutches. But seeing Carrie standing, walking slowly around the house, had made their hearts lift. Then slowly, little by little, Carrie began leaving the braces off. "My arms hurt." She made excuses. "Why bother? I'm more comfortable in the wheelchair."

Carrie didn't get out of the wheelchair any more, except to go to bed, or to sit on the couch, but whenever she moved, it was while sitting in the chair. Sewing in the basement, sitting in the wheelchair, Carrie had become a silent figure in the house.

Sandy stood there watching her sister busily sorting the sewing on her lap. She remembered Carrie's enthusiasm as she had sewed the curtains for their bedroom and then the bedspreads to match.

And when aunts and uncles had come to visit, it was Carrie who was the center of attention, playing with the younger children, and listening to the aunts' chatter, playing peacemaker and entertainer and anything else that the day called for.

Where had all the enthusiasm gone? Why had Carrie become so quiet?

"Carrie, it was really so exciting." Sandy bent down by the chair and draped her apron over the arm. "But at the end. . . ." Sandy shivered.

"What happened?" Carrie looked up. "Here, help me thread this needle." She handed the needle to Sandy and folded up the hem of a skirt.

"Well." Sandy licked the thread, then closed one eye and squinted, peering into the tiny hole in front of her. "There was a fight on the court. One of the players had a hold on another one's throat. Nobody could get them apart."

"It sounds like a rough game." Mrs. Dennis basted the golden-brown chicken roasting in the oven. "Carrie, do you want to make the salad?" she asked.

Carrie put her sewing down on the kitchen chair and wheeled over to the counter. She put the salad bowl in her lap, and then the lettuce and tomatoes in the bowl. She wheeled over to the table and began to shred the lettuce. "When will Dad be home?"

"Any minute," her mother answered.

"Good." Sandy pushed her hair back off her shoulders as she glanced in the small mirror hanging by the kitchen doorway. "I have a date tonight . . . early."

Carrie finished the salad, then rolled over to the glass doors in the kitchen and slid them open. The grass, growing limp and pale from the cool fall air, tickled her ankles as she pushed the chair slowly across the backyard.

"Where are you going?" Mrs. Dennis called from the house.

"Want me to come?" Sandy offered.

Carrie waved her off. "No. I'll just be gone a couple of minutes."

She guided the chair down the driveway and onto the sidewalk. The night was still with everyone cleared off the sidewalks and inside, eating dinner. Carrie didn't do this much, wheel by herself. There was always her mother or father or, of course, Sandy, or Sandy's countless friends who would always volunteer, "We'll push you Carrie. Where do you want to go?"

Twenty-one and never really out alone.

"You clod. You idiot. You dope." Carrie muttered angrily to herself as her slim hands tugged at the wheels, pushing them up the hill. Her voice was bitter and only the night air heard it. Her parents, and her sister would have questioned, "That can't be Carrie, not an angry Carrie."

Twenty-one and sewing in the basement in a curtained room with people coming and going, but she herself never really being able to go. She remembered how she had hated sewing at the beginning. She had wanted to work in an office. But the reactions around her each time she mentioned it had made her feel that perhaps she was foolish indeed to think that she could ever go out to work.

Besides, there seemed to be no real reason to go out. Everything had been brought in so conveniently. There was plenty to do in the house, food to eat, people to see and to talk to, and slowly the office dream had faded and the sewing machine, so handily there, had taken its place.

"We'll take care of you, Carrie," the words came floating back, and anger, new to the softness, the gentility that had always been Carrie, crept into her arms and hands as she struggled up the hill. She had never gone this far up by herself before. But now, though she was sweating and her arms ached, it seemed important just to reach the top.

At last she stopped, out of breath, at the top of the hill. She looked down with a sense of pride. Beneath her lay the valley, the house she had lived in when she ran and played in the backyard and slid down slides and pushed the swings high to the sky, pushing her legs to the tops of the trees. The same house that had seen her stop walking, stop swinging, stop . . . stop. Most of the same people still lived around them, nice kindly people who had filled her life and hours.

Filled them. But with what? With borrowed conversation, with borrowed living. But what about what belonged to her, the sewing on her lap, setting the table, drying the dishes, company in the basement?

From the top of the hill, Carrie could see past the valley down into the city. Her parents took her for many rides through the city. She loved looking out of the car windows. And sometimes they would take her in her wheelchair for a trip through the department stores, but they were usually crowded and her mother would end up by saying, "I'll get you what you need next week, when it isn't so busy." Then back into the car to watch and look.

From where she sat now, she could see her mother pull the drapes shut in the living room. The front light went on under the carport. Her father's car pulled up into their driveway.

Carrie watched it as she would have a movie. Everyone's in there, she thought, but me, but Carrie. Her mother would kiss Carrie's father hello. Her father would tug at Sandy's long hair and say, "Hi, sweetie," then look for Carrie down in the basement. "Kitten, I'm home," he'd call.

But Carrie wasn't in the basement tonight. She was up at the top of the hill. And she didn't want to go back. Not to the basement. Not to the house. Not to see Sandy getting ready for her date, not to watch her pinch her cheeks or fling her hair past her new date's shoulder, not to watch TV or sew or think . . . or anything.

But she had to go back. Because there were four dishes on the table and four forks and spoons and chairs, because "Kitten" had a place put aside for her, comfortable and cozy and warm. Carrie let go of the brakes on her wheelchair and the wheels began to spin down the hill. She forgot that she had been at the top, and that the incline was steeper than she had known. She forgot that the October rains had soaked the ground and that the mud was thick and slippery.

All she felt was the soft night wind on her cheeks as she let the wheelchair gain momentum, let it go its own way. Take me, she thought, you be the one to take me for a change, anywhere. I'll go.

She relaxed too much. The wheelchair edged toward the mud, then sank into it and Carrie felt herself toppling forward. Frantically she reached out to grab on to something, to someone, but there was nothing there but air and then mud on her face and hands as she fell onto the grass.

The mud was on her hands, in her mouth, and darkening the ends of her hair. Out of breath, and straining, she pushed herself up. Her legs curled under her, clinging stubbornly to the cold dampness beneath her.

A car pulled up to the curb. She didn't look up. She heard the feet rushing toward her, but tears stung at her eyes and embarrassment kept her face riveted downward.

She felt arms, strong, but gentle, lift her up and place her in the chair and then, feeling the safeness of the wheelchair around her, she looked up. "Thank you," she said.

Two elderly faces . . . a man's and woman's stared back at her.

"Are you all right?" they asked.

Carrie nodded, the mud caking around her face. "I can get home from here by myself."

The two faces smiled back sympathetically and disappeared into the car.

When she entered the kitchen all conversation stopped.

"Carrie." Sandy ran over to her first. "What happened?"

And then her mother, "Are you hurt?" with gentle hands wiping away the bits of mud still clinging to her.

And then her father, "What were you doing out there?"

Carrie sat there for a long moment, looking at the three people closest to her in the whole world. Suddenly she didn't feel close to them at all. She felt trapped . . . trapped inside the circle that they formed standing around her.

"What was I doing out there?" She turned and looked at her father. "I went to the top of the hill," she said with pride. Then she shoved her wheelchair through the circle they formed, forcing them apart.

"Aren't you going to eat?"

"Carrie, let us help you get clean."

"Carrie, we would have taken you up there. It would have been easier."

Carrie wheeled away. She didn't want them to see her tears. She was sick of it being easy. Somehow being easy didn't seem like living. But where was living? It wasn't at the top of the hill.

Where then . . . where?

· · · CHAPTER 3

Glen unzipped his jacket and sat back in the swivel chair, the plans in the folder spread before him. His team, the Zippers, was three years old now. He had nursed them through the rough times, watched them come closer and closer to the championship in the Nationals; he had groomed his basketball team from a group of floundering wheelchair players to a team of possible pros. He had encouraged them to practice, shook his head at their signs of defeat, angered them with his insistence that they push, that they work to be the best.

Glen had a dream. Now, sitting in the center of the city council, with the men in dark suits huddled at the far end of the table, the dream seemed to be getting closer, so close in fact that his heart beat faster at the thought of it. He had waited so long for this morning.

"Well, Glen, how about showing us the plans."

The councilmen turned toward him.

"Sure . . . sure," he said eagerly. He dipped into the folder and pulled out a stack of papers.

"What do you have in mind?" Jim Mazer leaned over toward Glen, a polite smile on his face. He was the head of the Shady Hollow City Council. He owned the biggest department store in town, and most of what was done in Shady Hollow was done because he wanted it done . . . or because he did it himself. He was basically a fair man, doing much to improve the town. Mazer fought until the local factories had installed smoke screens and filters, and the sky had turned from pink to clear blue again. He had been behind the committee to build the new school. And now Glen's dream. It was Jim Mazer who had said, "We'll hear you out."

We'll hear you out. They had heard him out before, when he had asked them to let his team use some of the school gyms for practice. But then they had answered with, "The wheelchairs will mark the floors," and, "We're all booked up with regular basketball." They had heard him out whenever he had campaigned for wheelchair sports . . . whenever he was looking for outdoor facilities to practice on for field and track . . . whenever he tried to make arrangements for the swimming pools so that his girls could work out. Eventually they got a place but the fight . . . always the fight . . . and, "We'll hear you out!"

He handed some of the papers to each of the men sitting around the table.

"Here's my dream," he wanted to say. "Make it come true." But he remained quiet. Don't push, he reminded himself.

"Is it a rehabilitation center?" someone asked.

"No, more of an all-purpose center."

"It's quite an energetic plan," someone commented from the far end of the table.

They went over it slowly . . . field house to include basketball and all racing and field events.

"Every team needs a court," Glen explained.

"Locker rooms, showers, pool," someone noted.

"Swimming is necessary to paraplegics. The competition in the Nationals is steep. The more facilities, the better the chances to practice and work out."

"Lobby and recreation area," a thin man with piercing eyes noted at the end of the table.

"And then, of course, an administration office," Glen pointed out. "We'd have a library, including study carrels, work or discussion room and a music library.

"The club rooms would be turned into dorms during games," Glen explained.

"I see there's quite an area drawn up for TV, cards, meetings, classrooms." Jim Mazer used his pen to point out the area to the man next to him. "And a place for chair repairs and storage?" he questioned.

"Equipment is a big factor with us," Glen patiently pointed out. "Bolts and screws and parts are always coming off wheelchairs, and we have extra wheelchairs in case of breakage. The stuff has to be kept someplace."

"A kitchen?" someone questioned.

"Of course," Glen answered, "on the other side of

the building." Glen found himself leaning over the big table with excitement, pointing out the elaborate plans to the committee.

"The gym would be huge. There would have to be a large circulation area around the athletic facilities for spectators and refreshment stands. Wherever there are wheelchairs, there must be plenty of room. Some of our biggest problems," Glen explained, "occur when we play in a small gym and the crowd is endangered by wheelchairs smashing into the walls."

"I see you have overnight facilities planned here." Jim Mazer's quiet voice came from the corner.

"When a new paraplegic comes to town, we'd like him to know he has a place to stay, until he gets himself adjusted, finds a job, meets some contacts. A new town is frightening enough. When you have to be aware of steps and boundaries . . . and, of course, people who don't understand, it can be bleak." Glen's face was flushed now. But the words tumbled from him easily, yet with a desperation.

"There'd be a bowling alley," he went on, "shuffle board, a chapel, a lecture hall for discussion groups and movies. And, of course, a place for display trophies. Public transportation would be accessible. If we had buses available, they would have lifts. And of course, a press room, when needed."

Glen's hands were going in every direction now, moving papers here and there, showing diagrams of the underground basement level, pointing out the absence of steps, the wide doorways, the halls that stretched generously from side to side, the bathroom facilities that were accessible to wheelchairs, the telephones, light switches, door knobs, all low and within a wheeler's reach.

At last the room grew silent.

"We'll have to give it some consideration." Jim Mazer put out his hand.

"Of course, of course." Glen smiled and zipped up his jacket. The meeting was over.

He shook their hands, each of them, and looked into the smiling faces, wondering if they really knew how important a center like this could be. Could people who walked ever really understand? *He* walked. But he had been with rehabilitation centers all his life, working first as a volunteer. Then came the four years obtaining a bachelor of science degree in physical therapy and after that the state boards, bringing him back to the rehab centers as a physical therapist. His hands, wanting to comfort, lifted, carried, encouraged, until his life seemed blended with all lives surrounded by wheels.

"This center would really cover a big area, Glen. There would even be a problem as to where to build it." Jim Mazer put his arm around Glen's shoulder as he led him to the door.

Glen looked up at him, his eyes filled with excitement. "Wherever it is, we'll have that figure right at the top of it, the figure of a para in a wheelchair holding a lantern, the symbol of wheelchair sports, the symbol of competition. It'll be so high," he raised his hands, "any paraplegic coming into this town will see it and know he's not alone."

Jim Mazer frowned. "It'll cost, Glen. The money is inconceivable. There will be problems."

Glen shrugged. "We're used to that," he said quietly and opened the door. Then looking back at the men, he smiled, as though he had a secret. "Take care of my dream," he said and closed the door behind him.

He went over to Bennie's apartment. The ramp in front, built by the coach of the wrestling team, was slick from ice. Glen picked up the bag of salt at the side of the door and poured it down the ramp. He hadn't seen Bennie in about two weeks. Winter was hard on wheelchairs, bringing with it slick ice, deep snow, skids, and tumbles. Glen rang the bell.

Bennie, guitar in lap, opened the door. He smiled and slapped Glen's hand as he walked in.

"Hey, man, enter."

"Brrrrr." Glen rubbed his hands together, walked straight into the kitchen, and put the kettle on.

"I put some salt on the ramp," he said. Bennie strummed his guitar, and hummed a soft calypso song as Glen took out some cups from the bottom pantry and set them on the table.

"You having problems?" Glen asked as he opened the tea. "I haven't seen you at practice."

Two Friday nights had passed, and Bennie had missed the basketball practice at the high school. Bennie, of all people, knew how crucial practice before the game could be. During the summer months, even when they weren't playing regular games, it was Bennie's idea to continue the Friday night practice sessions. "We got to be the best," he'd shout.

"Got to get out of here," Bennie answered.

"How come?"

"Landlord's daughter's moving in." Bennie put

down the guitar, resting it against the kitchen table. "She's been breaking it to me easy the last couple of weeks. Couldn't really think of basketball. Couldn't think of nothin'."

"That puts you in a spot." Glen made some tea when the kettle boiled.

Bennie shrugged. "Have a month or so to move. Got any ideas?"

"I'll tell the rest of the team. We'll start looking."

Bennie's CB radio blared out from the living room. "Hey, I meant to ask you, can anyone work that set? I'd like to get one for my car." Glen sat down and drank his tea.

"All you need is a twenty-dollar license. A Citizen Band radio would be great for you. You really don't need any technical knowledge . . . there's no morse code involved . . . strictly short-range voice communication." Bennie wheeled over to the set. "Blue here." He answered in his nickname. Only those involved in CB radio knew him by "Blue."

Glen went over to the library that Bennie had lining the walls. He loved this place, because Bennie was all over it. His CB radio, the books that showed his curiosity about every facet of life, the way he could take apart and put together anything that had wires in it, the way he could even restring his guitar. They all marked Bennie's curiosity about life, his ability to reason out what he didn't already know. On one shelf were several light bulbs.

"Need any?" Bennie called from the set.

"Yeah." Glen took a box. "How's business?"

Bennie shrugged. "If you like light bulbs, it's fine."

Glen knew what he meant. The knife wound he had received had curtailed Bennie's thoughts of an athletic scholarship to college. But it hadn't stopped Bennie. He had studied electronics while in the hospital, because even as a boy, he had told Glen, he had a way of putting wires together to make them work. He had hungrily read the books on his own during those long hospital nights when the hours seemed to suffocate him and only the reading, only the knowledge he was acquiring, kept him going. And then the year at Bucks Rehabilitation Center where he passed his test as a first-class electronic technician, able to repair TV, radio, and just about anything. else in the communications field.

He had made the rounds of the repair shops when he came to Shady Hollow looking for work. But somehow no one seemed to see him or even listen to his qualifications. All they saw was the wheelchair. And, like shutters closing on a windy night, the doors began to close, one after another, in his face. Glen knew that Bennie was waiting for the day when he could actually work at the craft he had chosen.

As if he had read his thoughts, Bennie wheeled over and asked, "Do you remember the day I first came out here?" Bennie picked his guitar up from the floor and strummed softly, as if the guitar were remembering too. He had met Buddy, one of the team members of the Zippers, at the Bucks Rehab Center. Buddy had told him of the Zippers and their sports team in a small town called Shady Hollow. The idea had appealed to Bennie from the start. He had spent many hours playing baseball in the overly crowded streets in front of his house. There were too many cars in the streets, too many people in the houses, too many voices trying to be heard, but he always recalled his neighborhood with affection because it was a together kind of place and there was always room for baseball. The knife wound in the alley was "just part of the breaks."

After passing his electronics test at Bucks, he packed up his things, put them in Buddy's car, and began his journey to Shady Hollow.

Glen found himself humming to Bennie's music, his body swaying slowly to the relaxing tones. He remembered the night that he had opened the door and there sat Bennie, as had so many Bennies before him, with his suitcase on his lap, and the guitar resting on top of the case.

Glen's dream of the center had stemmed from all the Bennies who had come to him over the years. Bennies who had grown tired of watching behind windows, who had become frustrated with their surroundings, tired of being turned down for employment, fed up with public attitudes and platitudes. They would come from all over, from rehabilitation centers, from private homes, from living in trailers, and they would hang their hopes on wheelchair sports, on the group of people involved in living the way it was possible to live, in excelling where they had a chance to excel.

"Be ready for the game next week," Glen said as he got up and wrapped his scarf around his neck. "It's a big one. We stand a chance for the championship, if we keep our heads through the season."

Bennie smiled. He knew Glen was referring to Skip's temper, even to Bennie when he lost his cool and spilled on the floor, forgetting that balance was urgent in his case.

"Don't worry," Bennie said, "we'll wrap it up." The winter seemed to be passing all too rapidly now for Bennie. With League games scheduled every couple of weeks and exhibition games to raise money sandwiched in between, the Zippers would finish up their season some time in April. Yet, even though it was now early November, the scheduled games ahead gave Bennie a breathless feeling, as if the calendar pages hung on his refrigerator would drop off quicker than he could handle.

A voice called out from his CB set. Bennie wheeled over to it. He put on his earphones so as not to disturb anybody else in the apartment house. He had been working the set for a year now. When he had been in high school, he had belonged to the ham radio club and had earned his ticket. Then came the year of silence and thinking, the blotted-out time of his life. But when he came to Shady Hollow, he was able to work out a good deal with a man who had an old CB set and was buying a new one. "Break Channel 11. Anybody awake out there?" the voice repeated.

The voice on the set was unfamiliar to him.

His face was set in a deep frown as he tuned in the set louder.

"What is it?" Glen asked, watching as Bennie wrote down the message.

He handed the slip of paper to Glen. "I need someone to talk to," it read.

"Better answer." Glen started to leave. "It sounds like trouble."

Bennie nodded and went back to the set. He sat

there for a second, looking up at the racks of books about electronics, the light bulbs stacked in the corner.

"So you need someone to talk to," Bennie said quietly. He heard the door close behind him as Glen left. He looked at the little radio still repeating the urgent message. "Who doesn't," he muttered to himself, and then in a clear, strong voice he answered, "Blue here. What's your handle?"

"I'm known as Black Diamond," answered the uncertain voice at the other end.

· · · **CHAPTER 4**

The blues and greens of the cheerleader's uniforms dotted the court as the girls went through their routines before the game. Skip sat by the benches, watching the long legs perform their acrobatic tricks before him. This was the first time the cheerleaders had ever performed for a wheelchair basketball game. Leave it to Glen. He had worked it out with the principal of the school.

The high school, the biggest in Shady Hollow, had just built a new gymnasium to equal the beautiful sprawling school. The Zippers considered themselves lucky to be able to practice and play a game now and then here. Most superintendents with new gyms cringed at the thought of wheelchairs streaking across them, but Jim Mazer had used his influence. The school was in Jim's section of town, the better section, where the homes had just the right amount of cars in front of them, and just the right number of trees framing the streets.

Skip couldn't help but compare it to his high school. It had been small. The toilets didn't work right, the stairs outdated themselves and bent to the unending stream of footsteps that had for years and years run continuously up and down them. The homes around his school were old homes, but strong ones, with wide porches and enclosed backyards, two-storied homes with tiny attics at the top. Skip had once felt secure in the old school, secure in the strong house that stretched up to the telephone pole in front of it. Somewhere back there, before Vietnam, he had loved running up the long front steps of the stoop, knowing upstairs were Mom and Dad and maybe his married sister and kids over for dinner.

Now things were different. Now he spent many nights in the attic with the tiny window, not caring to talk with his mother or father or sister, or anyone else. Just alone. Alone was the best way. It meant not talking, not giving, not trying to understand how he could have his leg one minute, have it disappear the next. Now and then Bennie would come to visit and they would sit out in front of the house. There was something about the way he played the guitar, something about the way he lived his life that soothed Skip.

"Hi." Golden hair flashed before him as a blue and green skirt swished by his wheelchair.

He remembered the last match; the tight hold on Kelly's neck, the golden hair.

The girl smiled. He felt the smile go through him. She was put together just right with long legs and long hair and a smile that made her blue eyes deepen. Even freckles right on the tip of her nose.

"Some school," Skip commented. "Delux."

"I'm still getting used to it." She sat down on the bench beside him. "I'm a senior and the school still seems just a couple of miles too long for me."

He looked at her. About seventeen, he guessed. He felt more than two years older than her.

"I graduated from Bishop High."

"Oh, that's near the playground." Her face dimpled.

He nodded.

"I saw you in your last game. I was really so glad your team won."

He cringed. He didn't want to remember. Winning yes. Joe Kelly no.

"Hey, Skip, here's your jacket." Bennie came out of the locker room with jackets piled high in his lap.

Skip jumped out of the wheelchair and grabbed a pile and began to give them out to the rest of the team.

He saw the surprised look on the girl's face. The name Sandy was scrawled across the front of her green blouse.

"Don't let it shake you, Sandy." Skip put his jacket on. "I can walk."

Her cheeks flushed. "I know . . . but I thought in order to play. . . ."

"Amputees are qualified."

Her eyes shot down to his legs. She couldn't help it. "You walk so well. I mean, I couldn't tell." She was embarrassed, clearly out of it, her face flushing even more.

He smiled, inwardly proud. She couldn't tell. She didn't notice his limp. Only he knew of the months he had spent in the bedroom putting the leg on, taking it off, covering it with a blanket on those cold winter nights when the cold of it in the morning shook every nerve in his body. She couldn't know of the hours of practice, of straining, of determination to come away with as little of a limp as possible. The doctors had said, "Don't rush it." He couldn't wait.

Her surprise was sincere. He could feel that. Maybe he had done better than he had thought. But now that she knew, she'd look a little harder for the limp. Maybe.

"I brought my sister Carrie today." Sandy pointed to a small, pretty girl, with short red hair, sitting in a wheelchair off to the side.

"An accident?" Skip asked.

"Polio."

He nodded, understanding. There were quite a few polio members of the Zippers. Some of them, just paralyzed in one leg or on one side, could walk with braces and crutches. Others, with more of their body affected, had to use wheelchairs to get around, such as paras and quadriplegics. The quads, with paralysis of both arms and legs, had a heavier load to carry. Skip was always surprised at the life some of the quads led. With little use of arms and hands, some were still free and independent. Many had a courage he felt he didn't have.

"Did Carrie ever see a game before?" Skip asked.

"No."

"She'll be surprised."

"*I* was," Sandy smiled.

The whistle blew, and Skip started to move off.

"Hey, good luck," Sandy called after him.

He smiled back. Smiles were cheap. He could spare it. Then he whirled the wheelchair around, almost in anger, and went out on the court.

The first half of the game was a massacre. The Zippers were clearly out-classed playing against the League's champions. Ball after ball was blocked, lost, or intercepted. Buddy became so nervous he didn't even fall. He just kept tipping forward, and always, Skip came to his rescue, tugging at the chair from behind and setting him upright on the court. But there was barely time even to help one another. And help was what they needed. A bolt from Bennie's chair came loose. And Jim's tire went flat. Another chair was hurriedly brought in. Sandy watched, again amazed that there was so much going on besides the game of basketball. The other team was clearly in command. Their setups were precise. They kept the Zippers out of the key most of the time and were under the basket for any rebound plays. Sandy left the other cheerleaders and walked over to where her sister sat.

"How do you like it, Carrie?"

Carrie sat there quietly watching. She had never really seen so many wheelchairs at one time. Now and then, going down the street, she would see one being pushed. But this! Flying wheelchairs banging into one another, paraplegics spilling out on the floor, nobody leading them or pushing them, just fierce strength, such as she had never seen before. Instantly she felt like one of them. Though she hadn't spoken to any of them, though they probably didn't even know she existed, she was one of them. This she couldn't tell Sandy. For Sandy could never understand.

"I never would have believed it," she said at last.

Sandy kneeled beside her. "I want you to meet someone on the team. Number 24. Skip."

"He doesn't even look like anything is wrong with him."

"He's an amputee," Sandy explained.

The whistle blew for half time. "Have to go. It's our time now. Come on over and sit near the team." Before Carrie could answer, Sandy pushed the chair with Carrie in it and she joined the Zippers.

The other teammates gathered around the basketball team, the girls chattering, giving the basketball players drinks from the canteens they had brought, wiping their backs with towels.

"Come on, Sandy." The cheerleaders were already on the center of the floor.

"I've got to run," Sandy whispered and she left Carrie sitting there.

Carrie watched her sister run out on the floor. She was clearly the prettiest one there . . . graceful . . . tall and full of rhythm. Even when she jumped to the cheers, her enthusiasm seemed to pale the others'.

"Is that your sister?"

A girl with a sweatshirt marked Zippers wheeled over to Carrie.

Carrie nodded yes.

"She's beautiful. Hey, do you live around here?"

"Yes, yes I do." Carrie tried looking over toward her sister. The girl's frank stare made her uncomfortable. It was the type of conversation she wasn't used to. Most people were casual with her.

"I'm Ina."

"Hi . . ." and then, shyly, "I'm Carrie."

"How did you get in there?" She patted the arms of the chair.

"Polio." So direct was the question it caught Carrie off guard.

Ina sensed the question in Carrie's eyes. "I'm a paraplegic . . . automobile accident." Then she laughed. "One thing about gimps. We all have a story."

A school band marched on to the court and the cheerleaders were hustled off to the side. The girls' band, with kilted skirts and big top hats, played and marched in gala procession around the gym.

"We usually don't have such great entertainment," Ina laughed. "This school really does it up right. Most of the time we're in a small gym with just our own squeaky voices to cheer them on."

Glen came over and squatted next to Carrie.

Ina's face lit up with affection. "Our coach, Carrie. The founder of the Zippers."

"The coach of the team who's flubbing this game," Glen frowned. "You interested in wheelchair sports, Carrie?"

"Oh, Glen," Ina winced. "Give the girl a second to catch her breath. You'll have to excuse him, Carrie. He grabs people off the street in wheelchairs and kidnaps them for the team."

Glen faked shock. "Only when we're desperate."

Carrie laughed. "I don't play basketball."

"But you're lovely and small and you'd be great at swimming. Have you ever done any swimming?" Glen asked.

Carrie shook her head no. "Not recently." There were many things on the list called "not recently." But she was almost ashamed to admit it. "Where do you swim?"

"At the pool here," Ina chimed in. "I'm on the swimming team."

"You have a swimming team, too?"

"We compete at the Nationals. I think you could really be an asset to the team, Carrie."

Carrie shrugged. She was confused. She had come just to watch a game, but now she had a feeling she was into something deeper.

"Why not give it a try?" Glen's voice was gentle. "We have a lot of first-time swimmers on our team."

His voice was soft, so understanding, it brought tears to Carrie's eyes. She knew he knew. She knew Ina knew. And because they knew all about wheelchairs, they knew about her life. Instinctively, they knew the nevers, the frustrations. She felt all pretenses leave her, the polite, right answers, the fake smiles, the not caring when she cared so. And suddenly her face was in her hands and warm tears washed her fingertips.

Glen's hand rumpled her hair.

"Oh, my." Carrie wiped her eyes dry. "I'm so ashamed. I don't know what happened to me."

Ina moved closer. "You don't have to apologize, Carrie, not for feeling."

"I have to get back to the team. I'll see you

later." Glen disappeared into the circle of basketball players.

And then the Zippers basketball team was on the court again, and Carrie and Ina and Glen began to yell and scream while the team fought for their last chance to come back in the game.

"You can do it." Carrie found herself outyelling even Ina.

"Come on . . . come on. . . . " Glen wrung the towels in his hands as point balanced point, but still the Flyers' lead was ten points and it was clear that the champions were not going to let this game get away.

"The Zippers are going to lose," Carrie said, disappointed.

"That's okay. We have six more games to play. And we stand a good chance even to come in second at the Middle Eastern League Championship. The first two League champions get a chance to go to the Regional Play-Offs in Ohio."

Number 24, Skip, was pushing hard. He seemed to use no caution when he raced across the court. Carrie looked at her sister whose eyes were riveted to him. There was a fierceness in him that frightened Carrie.

One of the players on the Flyers' team rammed Skip from the back. It knocked him out of his chair and instinctively he stood up. The whistle blew, for he had committed a foul by standing. But before he could turn around, another chair going at such a speed that it couldn't stop, rammed him from the side causing him to take a belly flop in the center of the floor.

He fell face down, stomach down, arms outstretched and the slap against the cement floor echoed around the gym. It took his breath away. For a moment he lay there stunned. It was definitely the most ungraceful spill he had ever taken. His head came up first . . . and there was Sandy, off to the side, looking over at him. He shook his head. He looked like a duck in a pool without water.

And then, when she saw he wasn't hurt, a small smile crept about Sandy's lips, and swelled into a giggle that turned into a rippling laugh. The cheerleaders caught the contagion of her laugh, and then Skip heard his own teammates laughing in the background.

"Hey, Skip, the swimming season's over," someone yelled from behind.

He got up smiling, at himself, at the absurdity of it all. He wasn't used to playing the clown, but somehow the anger that would have been there wasn't.

They got through the rest of the game the best they could. They lost, but they had played well, even at that. Skip's ribs hurt him and when he wheeled off the court, he stepped out of the wheelchair and rubbed his stomach, trying to massage away the soreness.

"I think we all need some food and conversation." Glen put his arm around Skip. "Get Bennie and the boys. We'll meet at the Snack Shop."

"Carrie, come on along, and bring your sister."

The Zippers soon crowded around Carrie. Introductions were informally passed around. Buddy shook hands. "Hi," Rosie called. "Hi Carrie . . . Hey Carrie . . . here carry this canteen for me. I'll drive you over," Buddy offered. "Skip, you take Sandy." Conversations like little bubbles floated through the air. But the only thing that Carrie really heard and remembered was, "Bring your sister along." How many times she had heard someone say to Sandy, "Sure, bring your sister along. We'd love to have Carrie. Of course it's no trouble."

How beautiful those words were now. How beautiful to know she was going somewhere at last . . . and yes . . . she would bring her sister along.

· · · CHAPTER 5

Bennie turned off the motor and sat in the car. He took a deep breath; his body felt tired from the long ride. He opened the car door, pulled his wheelchair out from the back seat, then opened the wheelchair and slid into it. He put on his gloves, locked up his car, then sat back for a moment, just looking at the rehabilitation center that stretched before him like a familiar friend. The January sky, filled with soft snow clouds, hovered over the center threateningly. Bennie hoped it wouldn't snow, not at least until they had returned home down those winding mountain roads.

A couple of cars away, Sandy was helping Skip pull some of the wheelchairs out from the back of the station wagon. There were ten cars altogether, ten parked cars filled with people who had come up to watch the game between the Zippers and the Bucks Rehab players.

It was like coming home. Most of the Zippers had stemmed from the rehab center, having left their homes to try to learn a craft or profession. This was the in-between step between home and the outside world. This was the place where sometimes you made it, or sometimes you didn't. The Zippers had been there at different times in their lives. Bucks was like the tree, and they the branches.

"Come on, Bennie," Sandy called and waved. "We're all set."

Bennie wheeled toward her. The cold wind pushed at the back of his chair. Sandy had become closely affiliated with the team lately. Bennie guessed partly because of Carrie, mostly because of Skip. Carrie still sat on the sidelines, two games now, during this past month, cautiously watching, not joining, but taking it all in. Bennie knew that feeling, that "not-believing-that-anything-like-this-could-exist" feeling.

"Here." Skip handed him the toolbox. "Fill that empty lap. Here Sandy, you take the uniforms." He stacked them high to her chin.

"Hey," she laughed. "You're suffocating me."

Skip looked at her. Bennie noticed the warmth in his eyes, something new for Skip. But there it was.

"Where's Carrie?" Sandy looked anxiously toward the parking lot for her sister.

"Buddy went in with her." Skip guided Sandy up the driveway. "He wanted to show her around a little."

"This is some place." Skip opened the wide glass doors as Sandy edged inside with the uniforms.

The lobby was large, wide enough for many wheelchairs end to end. There were benches, rows of them, to sit on, and endless corridors spreading out from the central lobby.

A boy lay on a stretcher-like table, his legs tilted, watching the traffic pass through the lobby. Midgets, paras of every nature, quads, edged their way in and out of the main lobby.

"Hey, Bennie." A smile lit up a face in the far corner. Bennie sped over and wrapped his arms around a bearded man.

"His roommate up here," Skip explained.

"Were you all here together?"

"No. I was just here for a year. Took a couple of courses but couldn't make up my mind what I felt like doing. Some of the Zippers," he pointed to Ina and Buddy and Mac, "met up here at some point. Come on. We have time until the game. I'll show you around."

They walked down the long corridors. Each room filled Skip's eyes with nostalgia. "This is where I learned to lift weights." The room was filled with weights and barbells. A big mirror stood at the end. "I spent many hours in here, alone, just training and aching all over."

Sandy put her hand on the tight muscle of his arm. He was so strong, built with such power on the outside, yet when he spoke of the past, especially here, his voice was filled with a tenderness that seemed strange coming from him.

"This is the recreation room . . . TV and chess."

They walked on toward a fountain with green plants circling it. Sitting in the midst of the plants, on the cement circle surrounding it, they looked at the trophy case covered by glass in front of them.

"Your team won so many trophies," said Sandy, recognizing the names of many of the Zippers.

He smiled, remembering. "We were the best." Suddenly Skip's eyes grew dark and cold. "I studied book-keeping here. The bookkeeping didn't matter beans to me. The government gives me a pension. So I shouldn't have a care in the world, should I? Come on." He grabbed her hand roughly, and with a slight limp, led her down the corridors. It was this abruptness, this sudden change of mood, that Sandy had grown accustomed to during these past months of knowing Skip. An inner understanding that even she couldn't explain, kept her from getting angry.

"Skip. Sandy! Wait for us!"

Buddy and Carrie had just turned the corner. "I'm exhausted!" Carrie was out of breath, her face flushed with excitement.

"Are you okay?" Sandy rushed over to her but Buddy gently nudged her aside.

"She's fine. Just getting some much-needed exercise. We've been taking a tour."

"Yeah. . . ." Carrie laughed. "He enjoys seeing me push."

"It's about time." Buddy tugged her wheelchair his way. "You can't have a free ride all your life."

Sandy felt out of it when the conversation turned like this. She could never have talked to Carrie this way; in fact, she never thought Carrie would want to be talked to this way. It was a tougher exchange than she was capable of having with her sister, for she loved her too much to dare hurt her. And yet, this didn't seem to be hurting her at all.

They had lunch in the gigantic lunchroom. Carrie went down the lunch line herself. Each wheeler had a walker accompany him so that the trays could be carried down the line. Carrie felt the first independence of her life when she found herself at a strange table with members of the rehab center.

"Are you with the Zippers?"

"Sort of," Carrie answered the girl next to her, who, though she seemed to have very little use of her hands, managed to eat her food unaided.

"They're a wild crew."

Carrie nodded in agreement.

"Been to Bucks before?"

"No."

"What rehab center are you from?"

"None." Carrie ate slowly, unsure of herself.

The girl looked up, surprised, noting that Carrie was obviously old enough to be on her own. "What do you do for a living?"

"I sew a little."

"Where do you live?"

"At home."

"I used to, too. My name's Jan. Come on, let me show you some of the classes."

They slid away from the table. Somehow food didn't seem important today. Carrie was so filled with the surprises behind each of the doors of the center, the people so active around her, most of them in wheelchairs, but moving so quickly, doing things, all kinds of things, and she was there to see it all.

They went into a section of the building that Buddy had pointed to during their earlier tour but said they didn't have time for then. Jan led her to the arts and crafts room with lines of pottery and ceramics lining the desks, then on into a small room that looked like a notions corner where socks, knickknacks, toiletries, and underwear were all for sale. "This is the small-business management course," Jan explained. "The center runs it as a course for people who are going into any business for themselves. It teaches them how to keep records of stock, inventory, and run a small shop."

Carrie felt chills go through her body. People in wheelchairs running their own businesses.

"Come on." Jan looked at her watch. "The game's going to start soon. I don't want to miss it."

They sped down the long corridors.

"Hey, you're going too fast," Carrie shouted.

"It's good practice. I work out for the Nationals down these corridors. Work up some good speed."

Everyone at the rehab center seemed to be doing two things at once, Carrie thought. Arts and crafts and racing. Small-business management courses and swimming. There seemed to be two dimensions to everything. She had come from a no-dimension world.

"Where have you been?" Sandy's worried face came from behind the basketballs she was carrying. Sandy was learning that being a walker with a wheelchair basketball team meant plenty of carrying.

"Here, put them on my lap," Carrie offered. She had found that the wheelchair had the capacity to hold other things besides herself. Cigarettes had been stuck in the middle of her wheel spokes and held there. Sweaters were slung over the side of the arms of her chair. She seemed to be in constant use whenever she was with the Zippers. "Jan, this is my sister Sandy."

Introductions were swift as the Zippers piled into the corridor. The basketball team was keyed up. It showed on their faces. They were playing their old alma mater. They were the boys who had made good and come back. Several of them started pulling off their shirts in the hallway, grabbing their uniforms as they sped into the gym. The locker rooms were small and the conversation was at a minimum as the Zippers hurried and changed.

As Carrie sat in the audience next to Glen, a coach from Bucks came up to him. He shook his hand warmly. "You son-of-a-gun. I hear you have plans for a miracle center."

Glen laughed. "It'll be a miracle if it comes about."

"Bigger than this and better?" the coach spread out his arms.

"It's going to be more than a rehab," Glen countered. "The works . . . every facet of a para's and quad's needs."

The coach shook his head. "I wish you luck, but it sounds like money, and you know what that word means."

It means no. Glen knew. There was money for curtains for a new gym. There was money for a new school to replace a school that was really not so bad. There was money for programs to investigate programs that investigated programs. But for paras . . . no money.

"Did you get some vets down here?" Glen asked.

The coach nodded and pointed off to the side. Some

young soldiers with nothing in the bottom of their chairs but empty pants legs sat waiting.

"They're tough to get out, Glen."

"I know. I imagine basketball doesn't hold much appeal for them after getting hit by a mine. But we'll show 'em."

There was more to their basketball games than just playing. It was showing the audience what could be done . . . that competition and skill need not be over because a person was confined to a wheelchair!

The rehab center had a basketball court that was accessible all the time to their team. This was to their advantage. The Zippers could practice only once a week at the Shady Hollow High School gym because the gym was not available to them at any other time. However, the Bucks team did not have consistency since members of the basketball team would come and go. Whenever they finished their courses at the center, they would leave the team. New members were constantly being added. The main group of Zippers had been together three years. Bennie and Skip were the newest members, having joined the team in the past year. The Zippers were now attuned to each other, knew each other's reactions, each other's weaknesses. They knew when to throw high to a teammate because of the extent of his disability, and when to throw low. They knew which player could move fast.

The game now in motion, the Zippers glided across the floor, out-maneuvering because they knew each other, playing from exhilaration, playing to win.

The final score was 50 to 35. The Zippers were

victorious, inching their way closer to the championship. Glen was ecstatic. Skip picked Sandy up and carried her across the court with a hoot. Ina and Buddy came over to Carrie.

"We're great," Ina beamed—"great . . . great . . . great."

The dinner at the rehab center was one of mixed emotions. Now it was good-bye time. Some of them might not get back to visit for quite awhile. The next game would be the following year. Some might not even come back then. The trip was such a long one, eight hours of driving over mountain roads. It meant, for those who had a job, taking time off from work, one day, maybe two.

The Zippers sat remembering the time at the center when they had felt safe, sheltered, when laughter seemed to have no limit, and learning was filled with excitement. It was a time when they actually thought the "outside" held jobs for them and involvement. So for a moment, they sat feeling safe, yet knowing the problems they left that morning, the problems of unemployment and frustration, were still waiting for them.

As they wheeled out of the main corridor, Bennie stopped suddenly by a closed door. "Hey, I haven't seen Shelly."

Skip turned the doorknob. Shelly, a quad, so physically handicapped that he was unable to feed himself, so sensitive, so introverted, so alone that anyone who had ever come to the center tried to warm his heart. Shelly always there, for years . . . and years. . . .

"He didn't make it," came a strange voice from inside the room. One of the instructors came out, his hands in his pocket, staring at the disbelieving faces before him.

"What happened?" Skip grabbed Sandy's hand as he listened and her hand hurt from being clenched so tightly.

"He drowned."

"But he couldn't move," Bennie protested.

"He had someone else do it. He got a retarded kid to tilt his wheelchair and dump him in the pool. The poor kid didn't realize what he was doing or know that Shelly wasn't able to swim."

The picture of the people who didn't make it grew clear and cold in front of the Zippers. There were memories of others who gave up, who didn't fly around the gym, who just couldn't fight anymore. A hush fell over the once-jubilant team as they slowly went down the corridor and out the front door of the center.

Carrie trailed behind by herself. She looked back once or twice at the closed door. A sudden fear crept through her whole being. Give up. She knew the feeling. She had felt it at the top of the hill . . . when she had spilled into the mud. She had felt it now and then, like a pointing finger, even before, when happiness seemed all around her, but none for her and her alone.

Who am I? she used to ask the wallpaper when she lay in bed at night. Where am I? What will I be?

The questions had overwhelmed her then. And frightened her so that she crept back into the safe cocoon of family and friends. But family wouldn't be there forever. And friends would come and go. She, Carrie, would be there . . . always.

"Wait for me," she shouted as she sped down the hall, calling to the Zippers ahead of her. "Oh, please, wait for me!"

· · · **CHAPTER 6**

Bennie and Glen sat in the small room adjoining the conference room. In the next room, behind closed doors, were Mazer and the boys. Glen had received the call just as he was about to go to the Brickton Home for Incurables where he was a physical therapist. Afterward he had sat quietly in his small apartment for several moments, knowing that the time had come.

He had called Bennie first, because he was so smooth, so cool and philosophical about life. "Bennie, would you go with me?"

Now, here they were again, on the brink, with the dream rolling around behind the shut door, where they couldn't even get at it to reach and help it along.

"What do you think?" Glen asked, his woolen cap clasped in his hands. "I mean, you really don't think they're going to go for it?"

Bennie shook his head. "I don't know, man. I just don't know."

They tried to talk of other things. "Did you find an apartment yet?"

Bennie shook his head. "Getting it at all ends from this town."

"What do you mean?"

"Are you black, they ask me? I think, they can't ask me that. But they do. I answer yes. And they hang up. And when it's okay to be black, I find I'm faced with the steps."

"When do you have to get out?"

Bennie crossed his arms and rested back in the wheelchair. "About another week."

Glen looked at him, amazed at his calm. "If you can't find anything, you'll stay at my place till you do."

"Man, you don't have the room." Glen didn't. His apartment was small, one bedroom, tiny kitchen, little living room. Yet people squeezed in, all the time, using it as an in-between place. Bennie shook his head. "Thanks anyway, but I'll get a place," he said with determination.

The door opened and the room buzzed with heated voices.

"Come on in." Jim Mazer led the way.

Glen smiled. "Take a deep breath, Bennie," he muttered. "We're going to get creamed."

He could tell by their faces. He had been turned down so many times before in so many ways by so many people that he knew by the look in their eyes, by the touch of their hands, by the way they put down their cigarettes. He knew it said no.

"Glen, it's a beautiful plan."

They always started out like that. Because it was the truth. What wasn't beautiful about a center that answered the needs of people in wheelchairs, needs of those like Bennie who now found himself threatened without having a place to live? A center would have seen to it that he found a ground-floor apartment without steps, and that he got a dormitory room at the center temporarily until he was placed. What wasn't beautiful about a center of intellectual and athletic pursuits, that acted as a springboard for the paraplegic and quad to enter life? He'd like to see any of these guys try it. He'd just bet their eyes would open if they had Bennie's view of the world.

"Glen, it's the money."

Bennie let out a slow hiss. That line was familiar to Bennie too. Throughout his younger years there was never enough money. He remembered the good breakfast served by his mother, and then the void till dinner. She never questioned where he got lunch. Sometimes it was stolen off the back of a fruit cart, an apple, an orange to stop the growl in his stomach; sometimes the owner of one of the grocery stores would throw a hunk of bread his way. But there was never money in his pocket to pay for it . . . and he was sorry for that. He was sorry he had to steal to stop his stomach from growling.

When it came to being rehabilitated, it was a little slower for him, a little harder than the guy who could afford the specialist, the extra nurses, and the home just set up right for him. They didn't have to tell him about money. At nineteen, it had been an important part of his entire life . . . the mere absence of it.

Glen shook his head. He wasn't really listening to Mazer. Bennie knew it.

Jim Mazer smiled gently. "It would take more backing than I have right now, and such an energetic concentration of funds to build this place that it overwhelmed me. The other council members agree."

The councilmen nodded, and smiled.

"The low public telephones on the side of the building." Mazer pointed to the diagram. "Great idea. I'd like to see it done in this town. And ramps built on the curbs. Might be a good idea to try."

"Might be," Glen repeated softly. He controlled the "might be." Has to be, he thought. Mazer wasn't ready for that yet. He wasn't ready for the young vets coming back from the service . . . or for the kids crushing themselves inside their cars. Might be. Tell them that.

"Look Glen, let me keep the plans. Let us sit on it for awhile."

A stall. Glen looked into Jim's eyes. They were polite eyes, experienced at this sort of thing. A slow letdown. Nice of him.

Glen shook his head. "Thanks for giving it some thought," he said.

Bennie put out his hand. "Keep cool, man," he smiled.

Back out in the corridor, Bennie talked of wheelchair sports to the man who had been involved in it for fourteen years. He talked of the track-and-field season soon to begin, of the first-place championship of the girls in the Nationals that had to be protected. But there was no fire in Glen's eyes, nothing caught at the flame.

Bennie's CB set was alive with a familiar voice when they entered his living room.

Bennie, recognizing the voice of Black Diamond, rushed over to the set.

"Are you there, Blue?" Over and over. "Are you there, Blue?"

Bennie keyed the mike. "Okay, man. Just got in."

"Someone new?" Glen asked as he peered over Bennie's shoulder.

"Remember the message, 'I need someone to talk to?' He's at the other end."

"Who is he?"

Bennie shrugged. "Won't tell me yet. Did you ever feel you've got someone hanging by a string and if you let go he'll disappear into nowhere? He just calls me every now and then. And we talk."

"About what?"

"Everything. The guy knows everything. History, stamps, magic, you name it. But he's got troubles."

"That's obvious by the first message." Glen put on his cap. "Thanks for coming with me, Bennie."

"Hold on. Let me sign off." He bent over the CB set and talked into the mike. "Get back to you later. 73s." Then he turned back toward Glen.

"It's going to happen, man. You know it. Some day it's going to be your way." Bennie took hold of his arm, trying to shake some reaction into the man before him.

"No." Glen shook his head. "I'm not in the chair, Bennie. Some day, it's going to be your way."

The door shut slowly and Bennie turned back to his desk. The telephone rang. He pulled the phone from the side drawer.

"Bennie here."

"This is Mrs. Jansen. My light bulbs never came."

"Sorry, ma'am. I'll check into it."

"Please do." The voice at the other end was sweet. Mrs. Jansen was a steady customer. She did her thing, ordering light bulbs three times a year. He knew she felt better knowing that the handicapped were working. It just so happened that he didn't really want to sell light bulbs and one day he might, instead of saying, yes ma'am, he might tell Mrs. Jansen he sure would like to fix her TV or her radio if it needed repairing, or make her tired toaster pop again. He might even ask her where he could find an employer who would realize his brain was still functioning though his legs weren't.

Functioning wasn't selling light bulbs. It wasn't his voice coming over the phone asking, "Would you like 40 watt, 60 watt, three-way?" It wasn't his voice. It was the voice of a stranger inside himself.

"Thanks for calling, Mrs. Jansen," he answered instead. "I wouldn't want you to be inconvenienced in any way." He needed the business.

The click of the phone ended the conversation.

Back to the CB set.

"Black Diamond, are you there?"

Bennie waited.

"You sure are busy." Black Diamond sounded irritated. "Every time we talk someone is either coming into your place or you've got a phone call."

Bennie laughed. "You might say I'm pretty active. I guess I just know a lot of people and do a lot of things."

"What things?"

"Well, this CB set for one thing. That keeps me pretty busy. And I collect stamps. You know that already. I'm also a member of a wheelchair basketball team."

There was a long silence at the other end.

"Are you there?" Bennie asked.

"I'm here," came the answer.

"Did someone come in?"

"No one ever comes in."

"Hey, what did I say? Didn't you ever know someone in a wheelchair?" Bennie tried joking. Another long silence.

"What's your bag, Black Diamond? Are we going to get down to it?"

Still silence.

"Are you finished broadcasting for the day?"

"Blue," one word came over.

"I'm here."

"I'm a quad. Catch you later. 73s."

The conversation ended. Bennie sat there stunned. Black Diamond was in a wheelchair too. But a quad, with arms and legs affected. There were some quads on the wheelchair sports team. He had watched them bowl with amazement. He had examined one of their bowling sticks recently. It was a simple instrument, a long stick with a scoop at the end to hold the ball in place while it was being pushed. It reminded Bennie of a shuffleboard stick, with the bottom like two hands cupped outward.

The stick was tied to the quad's hand so that he could use it to push the bowling balls down the alley. Once pushed, Bennie remembered how slowly the ball rolled down, for there was usually very little power behind the push. But the accuracy was the thing. Sometimes the ball would seem to take forever, and yet there would be a strike at the other end. The same with quads swimming at the Nationals. How many times Bennie had watched the quad swimmers laboriously inching their way across the pool, sometimes taking ten or fifteen minutes. Many times the audiences would stand up cheering at their unbelievable stamina and determination. He had watched quads who weren't supposed to be able to use their hands, use them eating potato chips, dialing phone numbers, typing, even writing. But Black Diamond, a quad who called out, "I need someone to talk to," obviously wasn't one of them. Bennie could picture him, just like so many quads, holed up in a room, protected or ignored, isolated or condemned. He had sensed the bitterness and defeat in the boy's voice. He sat there for a long time just staring at the little box in front of him. Familiar calls started coming in, calls from friends who were used to finding him home at this hour, beautiful people, some who had never seen him and whom he had never met, just touching with their special way of caring, reaching across the airwaves in a "hello, I'm here," kind of fashion.

He spent the day answering them back. Later that night, he turned off the set and wheeled to the window. He liked this place. He'd grown accustomed to the tall trees in front of the window, to hearing the footsteps going up and down the back stairs. He didn't want to move. But he had to. Two more days and he had to go somewhere. He felt so alone. Tonight he and the quad were one.

The next couple of days went by faster than Bennie would have liked. He spent hours making endless lists of telephone calls, keeping a note of landlords just to prove to himself it was true: that in the whole town of Shady Hollow, there wasn't a place for him to live.

Glen kept calling with tips that fell through. A trailer camp; Bennie couldn't afford it. An apartment; only to discover there were six steps in front.

"Stay here at my apartment," Ina offered on that very last day. "You can sleep on the pull-out couch in the living room until you find a place."

It wasn't unusual for the Zippers to share their apartments with whomever might be out of work or in need of a roof over their head. Especially Ina with her big heart. Many times Bennie had visited her and there, in the kitchen helping out, was a new face in a wheelchair. A girl from another city or perhaps even from a home for the incurable who had decided to take her chances on the outside. Until a job and a place to live were found, until the girl lost that terrible fear that comes with suddenly trying for independence, it was usually Ina who opened her door. Perhaps it was because she herself had come to the city from a farm where there was a big family, plenty to eat, and love that spilled over from family to friends.

"No thanks," Bennie finally answered. "It's really great of you . . . but I'll be okay."

He hung up.

He'd take care of himself. He didn't want to feel like

a load of freight, delivered to someone else's living room. Paraplegics were used to that but it had always been an inside fear to him, ever since he had been shipped from the alley to a hospital, then shipped to the rehab center. He had watched fellow patients who didn't have anyone who cared shipped to homes for incurables, and others shipped themselves to workshop shelters as though they were lifeless, meaningless, worn-out machines on their way to the junkyard. Inside those bodies, lights were burning, bright lights called minds, but nobody around saw them. He wouldn't be shipped. He would take care of himself.

Bennie spent the rest of the day packing his bags. He didn't have much. Books, his CB radio set, stamp collection, toolbox with all his things, his guitar, and of course, his light bulbs.

He piled the things slowly into the trunk of his car. He closed the trunk, then patted it tenderly and smiled to himself. He remembered that day in the used car lot. He had been driving by with Buddy when the blue car with the dent in the fender caught his eye. It was way off to the side, but there was something awesome about it.

"How much?" he had asked a guy with grease on his hands.

"One hundred dollars." Then, almost guiltily, "If you can make it work."

Bennie could. He had worked on it for weeks. Each time he repaired a radio for one of the Zippers or someone was referred to him and he picked up an extra repair job, he'd put the money in the car, fixing its broken parts as a doctor would have a patient, bit by bit, using all the skill he had acquired, and when the motor finally roared, it seemed almost like a thank you. The Vocational Rehabilitation Bureau had fitted the car with hand brakes which was the final touch.

So now it was just he and the car. Bennie slid over behind the steering wheel, folded his wheelchair, and put it in the back seat of the car.

He put on his gloves, turned the key, and let the car warm up.

Where to Bennie, he asked himself. How come you know so many people and you still don't know . . . where to?

··· CHAPTER 7

Here it was, February, the month Carrie had always dreaded. The excitement of the holidays was over. Spring was too far ahead to ever picture in her mind. In the past, February had always been a month where quietness hung like a heavy cloak about her, closing out all the light.

How different it was this year. Carrie sat at the edge of the pool, her heart pounding, not daring to look over at Sandy and Skip, who sat on the benches near the wall. She couldn't believe she was here. The last couple of weeks, she should have known, had been leading to this. She had attended several of the exhibition basketball games, the team meeting, and met so many more of the team members. Altogether, there were forty-eight members belonging to the Zippers. They had sipped coffee and talked, told her of their beginnings. So many had been just like herself, cared for and protected at home, unused to the world outside. And then had come the rehabilitation centers where they had learned to think for themselves, to study a craft, to feel like individuals again.

.Buddy had given her most of the support she needed. He had taken her under his wing. She had gone with him to the basketball practices each Friday and to the parties afterward.

She tried not to think of what her parents were feeling. The look in their eyes was one of fright and doubt. They still had not attended any of the basketball games. Glen had told her this wasn't unusual. Many parents of paraplegics in families similar to Carrie's, where the one in the wheelchair has been protected too much and exposed too little, refuse to accept the fact that there could be a life outside the house. It posed problems that the parents couldn't face. Carrie couldn't get over that. There was a problem that her parents couldn't face, but that she could!

"Carrie, be careful," they cautioned.

Of what, she wanted to ask. But instinctively she knew better than to open up the bag of doubts right away.

Did they think she wasn't ready for a life of her own? Buddy didn't think she'd have trouble.

"You've got to live away from your home for awhile,

Carrie." He had said that to her last night as they were leaving the bowling alley. "Either move in with another girl or go right into a rehab center . . . but break away."

It had seemed such a harsh statement that she had been silent all the way home, forgetting the exhilaration she had felt in the earlier part of the evening when she had thrown her first ball down the bowling alley. Break away. Could she do that? She didn't want to think of it.

She hadn't wanted to think of today, either. Swimming. It had made her shudder. She had done some swimming when she was a little girl, even right after polio, when her therapy demanded long swims in the pool. But then the swimming stopped. Just about everything stopped at the same time, so it had been years since she had been near the water.

"You really don't have to go," her mother had said that morning, noticing her nervousness. "Carrie, no one's making you do it."

"I want to," Carrie insisted stubbornly. For she was forcing herself. It was step number one.

Buddy wheeled over to the side of the pool. "I was waiting for Bennie. No one seems to know where he is. Have you seen him, Skip?" Buddy shouted.

Skip shrugged. "Not for a couple of days."

"We'll wait a couple of more minutes."

Several more members of the team wheeled over to the pool. Some slid out of their wheelchairs on to the edge of the pool and then into the water, squealing at the first shock of it.

Buddy saw Carrie's face grow pale.

"Scared?" He asked softly.

She shook her head yes.

"I know the feeling. Do you know I began to swim for the first time only a year ago. I hadn't been swimming since my accident and when I fell into that pool, I thought I didn't have any legs at all. I just could feel the top half of myself. It was terrible . . . just like half of me was there."

But Carrie did feel. That was the one difference between a polio victim and other paraplegics. Polio at least left you with sensation.

"What did you do?" Carrie asked.

"I sank. Went right down to the bottom."

Carrie shuddered. He put his hand on hers. "But I'm here, aren't I? So you know I came back up again. There were people on the side who would've helped me. But I didn't want any. I just kept sinking and coming back up until I got the hang of it and then I was off."

"Hey, Carrie, you're not going to learn how to swim sitting here on the side." Glen dropped the towels by her wheelchair and lifted her out of the chair. He set her gently on the side of the pool.

"We were waiting for Bennie," Buddy explained.

"Don't wait," said Glen, looking worried. "No one's heard from him for two days. He moved out of his place. Just drove off. I'm worried about that guy."

"Why wouldn't he let us help him?" Ina wheeled over.

Skip walked over with Sandy just behind him. The frightened look on her face as Carrie dabbled her toes in the water was impossible for her to conceal.

"I'll drive around later. I know some of his haunts," Skip offered. "We'll get him back."

"Carrie. I know you can swim. Sandy told us you

used to swim quite a bit." Glen took hold of her by the waist and slid her gently into the water. "Hold on to the side of the pool."

"But it was years ago that I swam." Her voice quivered. She didn't want it to. She was angry at herself. She didn't want anyone to know that she was shaking inside.

"Just remember," Glen went on, "to use the top part of your body. You're going to have to compensate for your legs. Your stroke is going to have to be stronger . . . straighter."

Carrie let go of the side of the pool for a second. She forgot, in a burst of enthusiasm, that she was over her head. She went under instantly. Just for a second. When she came up, she was sputtering, the water bubbling out of her mouth. Her red hair, clinging about her face, seemed on fire as the light above the pool shone down on her.

Sandy wanted to jump in and lift her out. She wanted to help her sister wipe away the fear that she saw on her face. She tugged at Skip's hand, a silent plea for him to do something. But he didn't move. Sandy started toward the edge of the pool, but Skip's strong arms grabbed her by the shoulders and pulled her back.

"Leave her alone, Sandy."

"But she's so frightened," Sandy whispered. "I can't stand to see her like that."

"She'll pull out of it."

Carrie clung to the side of the pool like a rag doll, out of breath, now and then looking helplessly toward them.

"Do you feel *anything*?" Sandy turned on Skip. "You

and your control. Deep down in you . . . do you really feel *anything*?"

His eyes turned cold on her. "What *you* feel isn't important now. If you can't stand it . . . leave."

Sandy gasped and turned her back on him. It was her sister, not his. That's why he didn't care. Delicate, sensitive Carrie. And they were all watching her, some from in the pool, the others on the outside, watching and not moving and leaving her there all alone. She didn't look back at the pool. Instead she looked up at the clock, hearing the voices from behind her.

"Come on, Carrie. Let go," Glen coaxed. "Let go of the sides and let me take you out." Glen stood behind her holding her under the shoulders, and Carrie let herself fall back away from the pool's edge and float with Glen's support.

An encouraging clap of hands came from the Zippers surrounding the pool.

"Relax, move your arms, I'm here," came Glen's reassuring voice as Carrie felt his strong arms guiding her toward the center of the pool. She was doing a back stroke now, feeling her arms push at the water, moving her as Glen's hand grew lighter underneath her. Still he didn't let go. Back and forth. Again and again. Each time Carrie's strokes were stronger. More certain.

A half hour passed, with Carrie gaining more confidence.

Ina called from the edge of the pool. "Come on, Carrie, try to swim toward me." Ina was only a few feet away.

Carrie looked up at Glen. He flipped her over in the water, so that she was on her stomach, but still held her. "I'm right here," he said.

She took a few strokes. He walked with her, his hands supporting her under her stomach.

"Let go," she said breathlessly.

Glen released her and Carrie's body, so long accustomed to the wheelchair, seemed free and spirited as she strove to reach Ina. It was just a couple of strokes, but then Ina's strong arms were around her, holding her, as Carrie caught her breath, laughing, trying to shout, crying, all at once.

"She did it," Sandy cried. "Oh, Skip. She did it." She threw her arms around him and only then did she see . . . there were tears in his eyes. He looked away quickly.

Carrie clung to Ina as though she were a life raft. She was tired now. She heard the cheers come up from around the pool as Ina helped her to the pool's edge.

"That's enough for today, Carrie." Glen helped her out onto the ledge in front of her wheelchair. "Next time, you can play the little fish. But you did well today, and the worst is over."

Carrie lifted herself back into her chair and Sandy rushed over and circled her with a big towel. "I'm so proud of you," she said, as she hugged her.

"You've got a lot of practicing to do, Carrie." Glen dried himself off. "Those girls you'll be competing with in the Nationals are sharp."

"This guy's always looking for points," Buddy laughed. "He sees a para, he automatically starts computing, how many points can that guy earn for our team?"

"None of us would be anywhere without him," Skip said softly. "We *are* because he's Glen."

"You really care for him," Sandy said, astonished that Skip would allow himself to care for anyone.

"I'd do anything for him. . . ."

She watched the dark eyes turn serious. To be cared for like that by Skip must be wonderful. He usually took people so casually.

Skip was turning twenty yet sometimes, such as now, when he grew thoughtful, Sandy felt he was much older. And then at times when he sped like a violent tornado across the court, he seemed like a little boy, with his hair whipping across his eyes, his cheeks flushed from excitement. But where did he hide those emotions when the cold, stonelike expression came over his face? And why did she care so? Why, indeed?

"I'd like my parents to meet you, Glen." Carrie put her hand on his elbow. "Can you come home with me for a few minutes?"

"Sure. I'll follow Skip when he takes you and Sandy home."

Glen was very seldom able to fit anyone else in his car. He usually got stuck with transporting all the extra wheelchairs and basketball equipment.

Carrie listened to Sandy's constant chatter as Skip guided the car skillfully through the late afternoon traffic. She had seen Bennie drive, and Ina, and so many of the Zippers. The thought of her driving her own car flashed before her, an unexpected picture, once a thought so preposterous it never would have existed and yet . . . yet, the pool had never existed either. Before today. What else was possible?

They pulled into the driveway. Sandy pulled out Carrie's wheelchair and opened it on the sidewalk beside the car door. Carrie slid into it with ease and a confidence she had never had before. She intercepted Glen as they reached the front door.

"My parents," she groped for words, "they're not too sure about. . . ." she stopped.

He made it easy for her. "I know," he said. "Wheelchair sports. They're afraid you'll get hurt, or disappointed."

She nodded her head. He knew.

"They don't want to let go, Carrie. And it's understandable. You've been their baby for twenty-one years, much longer than the average child. They've done for you for so many years. It's become a habit."

"They've been good to me."

"I know," he said. "But you've got to be good for yourself."

And then they went inside. And Carrie's parents, polite but reserved, served coffee and cake and listened to the excited recounting of Carrie's swimming experience.

"You should have seen her," Sandy exclaimed. "She was just beautiful."

Mr. and Mrs. Dennis didn't feel beautiful at all. Things had been changing so quickly for them in the last couple of months. First there was the boy with the limp, Skip, who was Sandy's constant companion, who didn't have a job and didn't seem to know where he was going, and who smiled much too little. Skip had a tough exterior that frightened them and a hold over Sandy that made them uneasy.

And now Carrie, Carrie whom they had been so sure of, was going off into the same crowd, risking her life in a pool, and chattering about going to New York! And this man Glen, appearing from nowhere, filling her head with impossible things. So they were polite but quiet. Glen read their eyes, and read trouble. Carrie, it's going to be tough for you, he thought, tough and maybe heart-breaking and maybe never. It depends on your strength.

He thanked them for the coffee and didn't stay long. Bennie was on his mind.

"You'll come to some of the events," he said before going. He knew they wouldn't. Not yet.

They said politely, "We'll try." They knew he didn't believe them. They wanted to try, but something inside stopped them. They had grown used to living with the idea that Carrie would never walk again. That had taken years. Years of feeling that there were things she could never do. They believed she could never do them. Now here was someone encouraging her. If she failed . . . they couldn't face that. Perhaps because they, too, would fail.

It was dusk when Glen drove home. A car was parked in front of his house. Bennie's car. Glen looked inside. Bennie was sleeping in the front seat. Glen knocked at the window.

Bennie opened a sleepy eye, then rolled down the window.

"Have you been lost?" Glen asked, angry but relieved.

"Just a little, man," Bennie answered quietly. "Been looking for a room and sleeping in the car . . . for two days."

"So why not for a week! I mean, just drive us up a wall with worry."

"I might have," Bennie answered wearily. "But then

I remembered." He put his hand on the CB set. "There's a quad out there who needs me. I got to hook up my set." And then he smiled his "I-got-control-of-the-world" smile and laughed softly. "Man," he said, "why does it have to be so rough?"

"Come in." Glen's invitation was more like an order. "That's the least you can do for me. Stay at my place so I know where you are. Then I can get some sleep." Glen rolled up his collar as the wind cut into his coat.

The first thing they took in was the CB set. The next thing was the guitar.

· · · CHAPTER 8

It had been a week now since Glen had taken Bennie in, a week of apartment hunting and rejections. Tonight, as the clock turned toward midnight, Bennie wondered just how long he could sleep in Glen's living room, how long his pride would let him. He heard Glen's comfortable snoring echo from the bedroom. Each night he had stayed up late, wondering if Black Diamond might call. Each night he found himself dozing off in the chair, just as now, wondering if he would ever hear from him again.

Bennie sat upright in the chair as the sound of Black Diamond's voice shot through the darkness. He turned on the light, pulled over to the set, put on the earphones, and answered, "Don't you sleep, Black Diamond?"

"Can't," came the answer.

"What's bothering you, man?"

"The empty room."

"Fill it up."

"Don't know how."

"People, man, people," Bennie said impatiently.

"They don't seem to see me."

"I've seen a lot of quads. I bowled with them, swum with them, and jived with them." Black Diamond had told him the last time they spoke that he had become a quad through an automobile accident. Bennie rubbed his forehead and thought a moment. The good words often came easily to him, but the last few days, he was aching himself. Now here was Black Diamond asking for help in the darkness of the night, and who does he come to? A guy who can't even find a place to hang his hat.

"Look Diamond, who do you live with?"

"My parents."

"They have a house?"

"Yes."

"Where do you fit in the house?"

"Upstairs in a room."

"Why upstairs? Man, you're away from it."

"They don't have to look at me up here," came the answer.

"Aw, come on," Bennie quipped.

"I'm fed, clothed. My needs are taken care of. I'm even visited."

"Don't you go out?" Bennie asked.

"What for?"

"Play it straight," cautioned Bennie.

"For walks . . . now and then . . . short walks." The voice was bitter.

"Hey, Diamond, you mad at me?"

"Where were you last week? I tried calling you for two days. Then I just gave up."

"You give up too easy. I've been having a problem."

"What's wrong?" There was concern in Black Diamond's voice.

"Can't find a place to live."

"My problem is I have a place to live, if you can call this living."

"Hey, Diamond, you busy this Saturday? Come on out to a basketball game. Let me know where you live. I'll get someone to pick you up."

Silence.

"No. . . ." came the answer ". . .not this week."

"I think you'd like the game."

"How come you can't find a place to live?"

Change of subject. Okay, Bennie thought. So you're not ready for it yet. "Wheels and color. What more could you ask."

"Got you," Black Diamond answered. "I'd like to say I'll see what I can do but I don't get around much."

"How'd you get so smart, then," Bennie joked.

"Mail-order courses . . . and lots of books. I spent so much time in hospitals that I learned to become quite a book reader."

"Yeah . . . lying flat on your back can improve your mind."

"It's the home for the incurables that really does it," Black Diamond confided. "That's when the world really closes in if you let it."

"Did you let it?"

"I kept plugging."

"How come you stopped?"

"Who said I stopped?"

"You sound like your motor stopped running." Bennie's words were like darts hitting the target. "Upstairs in a room. Man, that's being out of it."

Another silence.

"I can barely eat by myself."

"We'll teach you."

Bennie's eyes began to close. He was so tired. Two nights in a car hadn't done his back any good. His chest ached and his muscles felt tired. Glen's couch was better than the front seat of a car, but the springs were old and the couch was a little short for Bennie's long legs.

"How come you left the home?"

"I just couldn't stand it. My parents managed to keep me out of the house through most of the years, but now, there's no place else."

"You mean you didn't learn how to take care of yourself the whole time you were away?"

"No."

"Hey, Diamond, no kiddin', we got to get together."

"Maybe."

"When?"

"Sometime."

"Soon."

"I don't know."

"The game is Saturday night. Eight o'clock. Shady Hollow gym. Be there. Get your parents to take you, or the milkman, anyone! Come on man, shake loose. The automobile accident is over. You're a quad. Now get with it."

"73s, Blue." Black Diamond signed off in their code.

"Goodnight, Black Diamond, wherever you are."

Bennie turned off the lights and wheeled back to the couch. He looked out the window for a second. The night was black. A few small lights flickered in the distance.

A light suddenly lit the kitchen.

"Bennie? What are you doing up?" Glen called.

"Oh, just having a conversation with Black Diamond. Did I wake you?"

Glen shook his head. "No." He grabbed a bottle of milk from the icebox. "What do you think our chances are for first place in the League?"

"Could go either way. Maybe second."

"That's what I figured."

"Is that why you can't sleep?" Bennie wheeled into the kitchen.

"No." Glen's face was sad. "Mazer called today. He's mailing me back the plans for the center. You know it'll never be. They'll always ship it back to me and say, 'Tomorrow.'"

"It's a beautiful center," Bennie offered. "It'll happen." He wheeled over to Glen. "You've heard no before, man. Why has it got you down now?"

"Maybe I'm getting tired of trying to open people's eyes." Glen got up, put the bottle of milk back in the refrigerator and clicked off the light.

"It's all in front of everyone's eyes," Glen said in the darkness. "Why don't they see it?"

"Goodnight, Bennie."

"Peace."

· · · CHAPTER 9

Usually on the day of a game, Bennie tried to plan an easy day so that he was rested for that night. Two twenty-minute halves pushing in a wheelchair could drain a man easily. But this Saturday there was no time for resting. He had been staying with Glen two weeks now, and his search for an apartment was getting more urgent as each day went by. Today he knew he had to go apartment hunting again.

Steps, steps, steps. Bennie saw steps all day long, and small doorways. Where were the big old-fashioned houses, he thought as he wedged his way through one slim hallway after another. Now and then the apartments were just right. And nobody cared if he was black or green or blue. But then came the money. More than all the light bulbs he could sell.

He stayed out all day looking. The March winds blew at his back and fought for control of his wheelchair. It began to snow, and the wheelchair made tracks and skidded along the sidewalks as he rang doorbells and followed the ads in the papers. He stopped to buy some sweat socks in the five-and-dime and then, just as a last desperate attempt, he followed up on another ad for a room.

It was in a nice section of town, big houses, and lots of trees. Bennie had a thing for trees. In the city, there were smoke stacks and stacked buildings, but trees were at a premium. This place had them spread generously along the sidewalks.

He found the street and house, and pulled up. It looked like a place you could call home. Bennie tried not to think of it that way.

"Don't get your hopes up," he sighed to himself, got his wheelchair out and slid into it. The driveway was slick with the newly fallen snow and his chair skidded as he pushed his way up.

The side entrance to the house was flat, just right for a wheelchair.

"Hello." A woman answered the door.

"I'm answering your ad."

She hesitated.

"You did place an ad?" he asked.

"Oh, yes. Well . . . um, we just rented it."

He didn't believe her. She knew it.

Why did it have to be the ground floor and accessible? Why did the doorways have to look so wide? Why did it have to have trees and look like home? It wasn't.

"Thank you." Bennie turned away and pushed harder down the driveway. Because he was thinking so deeply about how it could have been, he didn't notice the edge of the curb. He didn't notice it until he spilled over in the driveway and his face hit the cold snow. A stillness filled the late afternoon and all Bennie heard was his quick breathing as he lay there for a long moment, face down in the snow, stunned by the cold of it. Slowly he turned himself over. He sat up and tried to slide back up into the wheelchair, but each time he pulled at the chair, it slid on the snow. So Bennie sat there, knowing he was getting his seat wet but not feeling it because he couldn't feel anything anyway from the waist down.

Two strong hands lifted him up. "Having trouble?" a voice asked.

"Thanks."

"My wife. You just spoke to her about a room. She called me when she saw you fall." The man had on his bedroom slippers. He shivered and rubbed his hands together.

"It must be tough in this weather for you." The man guided him carefully down the driveway.

Bennie shook his head. Falling out of chairs wasn't all that was tough. Snow wasn't tough. Snow falling gentle on the ground was clean and soothing. People, Bennie thought, man, people were the toughest. He slid into the car, folded up his wheelchair and slid it behind his seat into the back part of the car.

The man watched. "You really can do everything."

"Just about." Bennie smiled back. "Just about." He started the car.

"Good luck." The man waved.

Bennie waved back. His answer caught in his throat. He took a side road and drove on it for awhile, going nowhere in particular, his thoughts still whirling around a place to live. He didn't notice that his gas meter was running on empty. All he could think of was that he was running out of time. When the car stopped dead in the center of the road, he looked at the gas gauge, surprised.

Bennie rolled down his window. The snow was still falling lightly but about two inches had gathered already on the street. The road he had chosen was empty of other cars and only a dimly lit house a couple of hundred yards up the road stared back at him. He sat there for awhile, watching the snow fall, hoping that another car would pass him. He listened for the crunch of other tires on the street, looked in his mirror for something behind him, but only stillness and the house ahead remained.

"Well, you did it, buddy," Bennie said to himself. "So now undo it." He opened up the door, pulled his wheelchair from behind out onto the street and slid into it carefully. A wind stirred the snow about his face and bit at his lips. He locked the car and turned the wheelchair toward the lights from the house. On foot it looked like a ten-minute walk. But Bennie knew better from where he sat. He looked at his watch. It was five o'clock. Bennie pushed on the wheels of his chair. They slid and spun in the freshly fallen snow. Then, finally they took hold and began to turn. Why didn't he have a two-way radio in his car? Bennie thought about that as he pushed up the road. He knew the answer. He didn't have the money. Yet now, he could have used the radio to call for help. He thought about that, too, about no money, about no place to live, about the snow that seemed to fight him every inch of the way. At times he would stop and rub his hands together. Although he had gloves on, his hands were stiff and sudden pains shot through his fingers.

He pushed, stopped, pushed, breathing hard, wondering if the house ahead of him wasn't moving away, just to taunt him. At last the lights began to come closer and then he was in front of the house, staring at the long steps leading up to the front door. He just sat there breathing hard. And then in frustration, because he was angry at the road and the snow and the steps, he began to yell, "Hey you, inside, anybody home?" Over and over, "Hey, in there, can't you hear me?" but the wind, stronger now, swept his words away. At last he could yell no more.

He slid out of the chair and dragged himself up the steps. He counted them as he pulled himself up over one after the other, feeling the wet snow underneath him. And then his fists were pounding on the bottom of the door.

The door opened. A face looked down surprised. A man with white hair and a beard to match scratched his head, bent down and tried to lift Bennie up.

"No." Bennie waved him off and pointed to the wheelchair at the bottom of the steps. "Have you got any gas? I ran out of it and my car's stuck up the road."

"You out here by yourself?" The man was squatting now, so that he could see Bennie more clearly.

Bennie nodded his head. "Yeah," he answered. "All

by myself." Was the man afraid that perhaps Bennie was pretending . . . perhaps that there were others hiding in the snow? Distrust left the man's eyes and a cautious smile came to his lips. "I'll be right out," he said.

Bennie sat there on the porch for a moment shaking his head. He could have used a hot cup of coffee or a warm place to soothe his hands, but he knew it wouldn't be inside. Inside, there was distrust and perhaps fear. Even now as he sat there, he knew behind the windows, eyes peered at him, wondering.

He saw the curtains flutter by the window and guessed that he was right. Bennie edged his way to the top of the steps and slid slowly down them. He took a strong hold on the wheelchair, hoping that it wouldn't slide, turned and slid into it backwards. He breathed a sigh of relief as he rested back in the chair, waiting for the door to open again.

The white head showed through the open doorway. The man held a gasoline tank in his hand. He went over to the garage and drove his car down the driveway. Bennie met him at the street.

"How you going to get in?" The man looked out his opened window frowning. He obviously didn't have the slightest idea as to what to do with a wheelchair, a man in a wheelchair, a black man in a wheelchair. It was written all over his face. Bennie almost wanted to laugh. If he yelled boo . . . he just bet that man would drive away. Luckily, the man had a two-door car.

"I'll get in. Don't worry." Bennie opened the front door, slid out of his chair, closed the chair up, tilted forward and slid the wheelchair behind the front seat.

"Well, I'll be," came the voice next to him. "That's pretty clever."

Bennie didn't answer. He didn't feel clever. He had forgotten to check his gas tank. That wasn't clever.

In a couple of minutes, they reached Bennie's car. It had taken Bennie over forty-five minutes to wheel the distance to get gas. And just a couple of moments to return.

Bennie got in the car and the man poured the gas into the tank. Then he came over to Bennie's car window. Bennie pulled out some money from his wallet. But the man shook his head. "I really admire people like you," he said, "but I still don't think you should be let out by yourself."

The phrase "let out" froze in the air and sent a rod of anger through Bennie, but he smiled and said, "Thank you very much . . . for everything."

Only after the man was out of sight did his mouth turn grim as he repeated the words "let out." Then, remembering the basketball game at eight, he started the motor, and made a U turn in the road, driving away from the house he had never been in.

That night on the court, he felt tired. The whole team did. Some were working two shifts at jobs, some working during the day and attending school at night, while others were just suffering from the cold. The whole team was badly in need of spirit. They were not up to playing. They lost. Actually, they never stood a chance. They didn't pick up rebounds. Buddy kept falling out of his chair. The turnovers were unbelievable and, off to the side, the disappointed faces of Ina and Carrie, Glen and Sandy, all blended into a portrait called losing.

The game seemed like it would never end. The other team wasn't that good, but the way the Zippers were playing, they looked great. The Zippers were sloppy. They looked as if they didn't care.

Bennie felt that way. Tonight, basketball didn't seem important at all. Winning, which was always his thing, didn't seem to be where it was at. The day had taken a chunk out of him. So he and the team went through the process and the audience just got fed up with them.

Now and then Bennie's eyes would go over the crowd, looking for Black Diamond, looking for a quad. Ina waved to him. Glen yelled, "Get with it."

"Yeah . . . yeah. . . ." Bennie's face still hurt from the fall in the driveway. He remembered the house he could have called home. He remembered the house he had never been in. He missed the lay-up.

The horn sounded and the game was over. Bennie winced when he saw the score—60 to 25. This put them behind in the League and they had the last two tough games ahead. He wheeled over to the crowd and looked up at the benches.

No Black Diamond. He shook his head, disappointed. The gym emptied quickly. Only the Zippers remained in a small group.

Bennie picked up his guitar which sat propped up against Ina's wheelchair and began to strum. The sweet sound drifted throughout the gym and helped to mend the terrible night.

• • • CHAPTER 10

A spring centerpiece of flowers sat in the middle of the dining room table. The game had been held at one o'-clock in the Shady Hollow gym. By three o'clock, the Zippers were on their way to the celebration party at Ina's apartment. The three-week layoff that the Zippers had had since their last bad loss had done them a lot of good. That, and the fact that the day, though early in April, bore a strong hint of spring. The Zippers won. They were in first place for the League championship. There was one more game to play.

Carrie sat on the floor with her legs curled under her. Most of the Zippers were there. Ina had folded her chair, sliding onto the couch. Wheelchairs were stacked by the front door and to the sides of couches and chairs. It was a good feeling when a party was held in a house where someone understood about wheelchairs. Carrie felt free to relax on the floor, the others to plop on the furniture, or on pillows on the floor, leaning against their wheelchairs, using them as backrests.

There was a low table in the center of the room with pizza and soda. Carrie shut her eyes, listening to the talk, like music, around her. The last couple of months had been work, hard work, on her part. Ping-Pong and bowling. And swimming. She was swimming by herself now, without Glen's support. Glen was right. She had turned out to be one of the better swimmers on the team. Perhaps it was because her body had been still for so long. It seemed to break free in the water. She even attended an arts and crafts class now with Ina.

Carrie saw more and more of the Zippers, less and less of her parents. She seemed happiest away from home now and she couldn't quite put her finger on why. Perhaps it was because at home it was, "Carrie, let me do this," and "Don't hurt yourself," or "We'll do it for you," and "Daddy and I will take you."

The Zippers didn't do that to her. "Carrie, take care of it," they'd say. At first she'd panic. But then a look of reassurance from Buddy, or a smile from Sandy who was beginning to understand, and she would do it. She could swim that extra mile. She could bowl that extra game. Don't protect me, she kept trying to tell her parents. Protection was suffocation to her now.

Bennie sat off to the side in a corner of the room. He started to play his guitar. All his songs were sad lately. He was still apartment hunting and as much as the Zippers tried to help, there were feelings stirring inside Bennie now that only he could cope with. Last week he had wheeled as far as the bathroom in one place, only to find out he couldn't fit into it with the wheelchair. The alternative was placing a chair in the bathroom, then transferring from the wheelchair to the chair and so on. It just didn't pay, he had told Carrie, disappointedly.

He closed his eyes and sang, his voice low and soft. The Zippers quieted and listened. They hummed along with him, passing around the soda. There was a closeness in the room, a oneness, a world of its own that Carrie now felt part of. She saw Sandy in a corner with Skip, their heads bent together. Sandy's gaze, soft and loving . . . Skip still somewhere hidden in himself.

"Having a good time?" Buddy edged his way over.

Carrie nodded.

He handed her some pizza. "You put in a good hour of swimming this morning."

"I know. I wanted to get some extra practice in before the competitions start." She rubbed her shoulders.

"Sore?" he asked.

She nodded. "Ping-Pong and swimming. I'm growing muscles I never knew I had."

"Don't overdo it, midget," he smiled. "You said you had some shopping to do today."

Carrie remembered. "Oh, I guess it could wait." What she meant, the habit she had fallen into, was someone at home would take care of it.

"Well, if it's stuff you need, we can leave here a little early and I'll take you."

"Hey, great." Her big eyes opened wide with excitement. A surge of independence swept through her.

When the party slowed down a bit, Buddy and Carrie left quietly. It was an easy apartment to get out of. The halls were big and the door leading to the outside was without steps.

"Where to?" Buddy asked.

"Five-and-dime. They're open late tonight."

They stopped by a gas station on their way. "Hey, I noticed your tires look a little flat. How about getting some air for them?"

Carrie looked back at her wheelchair. Her father had always taken care of it for her. Somehow, mysteriously, he always managed to fill the tires up when she was sleeping or not using it. It never occurred to her to look after it herself.

Buddy slipped the wheelchair out of the back seat, gave it to the attendant. "Take care of the tires," he said.

"Sure," the attendant waved.

A few moments later, the wheelchair was again in the back seat.

"You've got a good wheelchair, Carrie. Better learn to take care of it," Buddy cautioned her as they drove out of the gas station.

They parked in front of the five-and-dime. Carrie slid her wheelchair out from the back seat on her side, then slid into it. Buddy did the same from his side. They met at the curb. "This time I'll help you up," he said, "but not next time." He tilted her chair back in a wheely and with a powerful thrust, pushed her up over the curb. She was on the sidewalk now.

Buddy noticed a bakery across the street. "I'm going to get some bread," he said. "Meet you in the five-and-dime."

He left her sitting in the wheelchair. "But," she protested, not knowing what to do. She had never been outside like this before, alone. She sat by the curb stunned. Her hands grew cold. Buddy disappeared into the bakery across the street without looking back.

Carrie turned her wheelchair around. She pushed herself up to the door of the dime store. It automatically opened. She breathed a sigh of relief. Slowly she edged her way down the aisles, looking over the counter at the colorful assortment of goods. She forgot what she had come for. Actually she was too excited just at being by herself . . . shopping. She began to relax. Buddy wasn't far away. There was no one at her elbow bending over her, suggesting, helping. She could take her time and think.

Carrie went up and down every aisle, fingering the plants, looking over everything, trying on hats. She peered into lipstick tubes and even ate a sample of chocolate lying on the scale at the candy counter.

She went over to the pet section and talked to the birds. The turtles made her grimace, but the fish tank held her spellbound. Black Mollies and guppies floated past her in blue green water, pursing their mouths and staring back agog.

Fish in a tank, birds in a cage. Suddenly Carrie felt sorry for them, sorry for anything that had a border around it. "May I help you?" an employee asked, noticing Carrie's red head bent deeply over the tank.

"Oh no," she laughed. "They're just so cute." And then she wheeled off, smiling to herself. What a beautiful store. What a beautiful day. Why in the world did people complain about shopping? She found it to be the wonder of all wonders. She was just choosing her first purchase, a pocketbook that would fit just beside her in the chair when a loud bang shot through the store.

Carrie dropped the bag. It sounded just like a gunshot had echoed across the ceiling of the store. Her heart began to beat faster. The other customers in the store looked around, startled.

And then again, another bang. Carrie felt her wheelchair sink. She looked down. "It's me," she said aloud. "My goodness, my tires!"

She had in fact two blowouts. The gas station attendent had obviously put too much air into the tires. She sat there stunned.

The manager of the store came over to Carrie. "You nearly caused a panic," he laughed. "I heard the noise up front."

"I'm so sorry." Carrie's face was crimson. She apologized for her tires, although she felt more frightened than ashamed. Where was Buddy? Why hadn't someone warned her about tires . . . and blowouts?

"Are you with someone?" the manager asked.

"Yes, he's in the bakery across the street."

Buddy's voice came from behind. "Hey, ma'am, you have a flat?"

She turned around, angry, almost blaming him. "Where have you been?"

"Eating cinnamon buns," he said and handed her one. She put it on her lap and helplessly put up her hands. "I'm stuck, Buddy."

"Have you got someone to help push her chair?" Buddy asked the manager.

The manager motioned to a stock boy who carefully pushed Carrie down the aisle, past the pet counter, the lipsticks, the hats.

"My new pocketbook," she sputtered.

She took out money and payed the woman at the cash register; then, with bag in hand, she let the stock boy's strength guide the chair out the front door and up to the car. Buddy wheeled behind. It was quite a job to push a wheelchair when the tires were flat. He was glad there was help around.

Carrie didn't say a word during the ride home. "Cat got your tongue?" Buddy finally asked as they neared her house.

"What would I have done if you weren't there?"

"Well, you would have to get out of there somehow. If you were driving your own car, you would have asked someone to help you to the car, just as they did today, and then driven home. Once home, you would have just wheeled yourself into the apartment as best you could. It would be difficult, but you could do it. And then, once you got inside, all you would have to do is pick up the phone and call a friend. They could help you pick up an extra wheelchair, maybe borrow one, until yours got fixed . . . and then you're back in business.

"Don't be ashamed to ask for help, Carrie. When you need it, turn around until you find a helping hand. When you're in trouble, learn to call out. And learn to get around on the floor whenever possible. There might be times when you'll have to."

Carrie didn't like the picture. She didn't like being stranded. She didn't know how to drive a car. She didn't know if she liked what it took to be independent.

"You really should learn to drive," he told her as

they pulled up into her driveway. He tooted the horn. Carrie's father came out.

"What's up, kids?" He peered into the car.

"Your daughter has two flats."

Mr. Dennis frowned. He knew something like this would happen. These scatterbrained Zippers seemed so reckless, so unaware of Carrie's sensitive needs. Carrie, pale and obviously shaken, let herself be carried in by her father.

He placed her gently on the couch. Then he went back out to the car and pulled out her wheelchair. "I have two new tires that I keep downstairs for emergencies." He gave Buddy an accusing look.

"She looked frightened," he said.

Buddy looked out through the opened car window, his green eyes squinting as the sun hit them. "Why didn't you tell her about blowouts?"

"She never had to know. I've always taken care of her wheelchair."

Buddy just shook his head. "I've got to get going," he said. "Tell her I'll be in touch."

Carrie watched her father carry the chair through the front doorway. He gave her a quick, reprimanding look, then went downstairs into the basement.

Her mother came down the stairs. "I was watching from the bedroom window. You really shouldn't be out so much."

"Why not?" Carrie asked.

"You look pale. You could get run down, catch cold."

"I bought a pocketbook." Carrie proudly pulled it out from her shopping bag.

"It's pretty," her mother said.

"Right now my shoulders hurt. I think I'd like a bath." Carrie rubbed the back of her neck.

"It's the swimming, isn't it?" her mother leaned toward Carrie, reaching out to touch her, but Carrie pulled away. She was confused. Nothing seemed right any more. Alone in that five-and-dime, she had wanted to die. Here, with comfort all around her, she felt alone.

Carrie's father carried her into the bathroom where she undressed. Her mother sat on the stool where she always sat when Carrie took a bath. "Are you ready?" her mother asked, getting some towels from the closet. Then with muscles trained and strengthened from years of lifting Carrie, she carried her over to the tub and placed her gently in the water.

Carrie sat in the tub watching the soapsuds swirl around her. Some day she would like to take a bath by herself. Some day she would like to close that door and sit with the soapsuds and her thoughts and close out the whole world. Her mother sat on the stool behind her.

"What is it, Carrie?" she asked softly.

Carrie didn't turn around. Here in this room, she didn't feel like the Carrie who had laughed, wheeling down the five-and-dime aisles.

"What is it Carrie?" The question was so simple. The answer even simpler. "I'd like to be able to take my own bath," she said quietly, her eyes shut.

· · · CHAPTER 11

The senior high gym was decorated for spring. Yellow-bright paper daffodils and red tulips hung from the ceiling. Forsythia was grouped colorfully in large vases placed in the corners of the room. Balloons and streamers, the colors of spring, tied and pasted to corners and ceiling, floated through the room, mingling with the flowers and other spring greenery.

Sandy looked around proudly. It had been a long afternoon of hard work, but her committee was determined to make this a dance that none of the seniors would forget. She stood there fingering one of the huge tulips. Usually, before a dance, she was filled with anticipation, for she loved to dance, loved the excitement that went along with gowns and music.

Tonight a cloud hung over her. She had asked Skip to be her date. He had hesitated for a moment too long. Then he had said, "Okay, sure."

She wanted to ask him why the smile had disappeared from his face the night she had invited him. She wanted to know why his eyes grew troubled and why he drove home in silence.

But she didn't dare. Because he might tell her. And she wasn't sure she could take it. She wasn't sure she could take half the thoughts that were on Skip's mind.

She had wanted him to pick her up at home, but someone had to be at the gym early to check things over, so they had arranged to meet here. Sandy was wearing a pale blue gown. Her hair hung long and straight about her shoulders and she swung a little white bag back and forth as she glanced up at the clock and waited impatiently.

She looked out toward the parking lot. Why did she think he wouldn't come? She had that feeling every time he was supposed to show up. After school. When he took her for a ride. When he appeared for a date, late, nonchalant, uncaring. She was never sure he would remember their date . . . or perhaps care enough to remember.

Sandy grabbed her sweater from the hanger near the front door and stepped outside. The parking lot was lit up as cars began to pull in and slowly fill it up. She watched the faces pass her by, talking classmates, holding each other's hands. Girls swished by in their long gowns. The hall behind her filled with excited faces, but not Skip's face.

She began to move her feet to the rhythm of the music from inside the gym. And then she saw him. Even though he was at the far end of the lot, she could see the slight limp, the tall lean body coming toward her.

She wanted to say, "You're late," when he finally was in front of her, but she stopped herself.

He didn't give any excuses, just smiled and took her elbow and led her into the gym, now filled with people. Skip looked around. "You did quite a job Sandy," he said proudly. "Did you work in here all day?"

Sandy nodded her head. "On ladders and the whole works. We looked like coal miners when we finally finished."

She led him over to one of the small tables in a corner of the gym.

"I had to work late tonight. Some of the bookkeeping down at the place had to be straightened out."

Sandy knew he didn't like his new job. He did some bookkeeping for one of the small grocery stores in the shopping center.

"Skip, is he treating you any better?"

"If you mean, did I get a raise, no."

"You could go to college."

"Why?" he asked.

Sandy hesitated. Was she going too far with him? She could never tell. Six months of attending all his games, of a now-and-then movie on Saturday night, of being by his side more than anyone else's and yet . . . he kept her outside of himself. And she was afraid to go any deeper. "You could teach," she said at last.

"That's your bag."

Sandy laughed. "There's room for another teacher in the bag."

"What are we playing," Skip asked her, "find a vocation for Skip?" He looked at her seriously. "I'm not thinking about tomorrow, Sandy. Today is where it's at with me. Today and now. When I get that straightened out, I'll take on tomorrow."

She had made him irritable. A silence fell between them. He could see by her face that he had hurt her.

"Look," he said gently, "I went into the army at seventeen. My parents gave me their consent, reluctantly, because I thought I knew what I was doing. I was over in Vietnam one month, Sandy, four weeks to the day, when I happened to put my foot down on the wrong patch of land. I still hear that explosion. Sometimes in the night, I think it's happening all over again."

"Skip, I didn't mean to. . . ."

"To open it up. Well, you did. So here it is. I spent over six months in a hospital, one year in a rehab center where I took up accounting courses, and now here I am . . . out . . . taking care of run-down books in a run-down grocery store. At seventeen, I thought I knew where I was going. Today, I honestly can say I don't know where I'm going and I don't care. Do I think of college? . . . sometimes. Do I think of the future? Sometimes. But most of the time, I think about that mine, and my leg, and everyone who said, 'Skip, you're now ready for the outside world,' except I'm not sure I am. Not yet."

"Aren't you two going to dance?" Some of Sandy's friends gathered around them. "Give her a break," one of them said to Skip.

Skip got up and took her on the dance floor. She had never danced with him. She wasn't sure he could. Why did I put him in this spot, she asked herself over and over as she felt him take her in his arms and begin to move to the music. He was stiff at first, but then he began to relax. The rhythm, so natural to his body, caught hold and he began to hum to the tune as he danced close to her.

He stepped on her foot. He didn't know it because he didn't feel it, but she did and winced. He looked at her. "Did I hurt you?" he asked.

"No."

"Come on." He took her hand and walked off the floor. "Enough punishment for tonight."

They sat at the table for a while, not having a very good time. Skip went back into himself, conscious of everyone on the dance floor, determined not to repeat his last performance.

"You really dance well," Sandy tried, for it was the truth. His body just felt the music and seemed to move instinctively with it.

"We'll try it in your garage next time," he answered sarcastically.

She tried talking about the game coming up.

"I have to get my leg fixed first," he said.

"What's wrong with it?"

"I have some sores. The leg has to be adjusted. I've lost some weight. That makes a difference in how a leg fits. Sometimes it can be done while you wait at the hospital, other times you have to leave the leg. Has to do with the plastic wood being baked."

"It sounds almost as complicated as taking care of a car." Sandy looked over at him.

He smiled. "No, not quite. But I do oil it sometimes, and I have to be careful of cold weather."

They began to like each other again, instead of fighting, with Sandy not having to climb over the brick wall that Skip kept setting up in front of himself. The rest of the dance went by quickly as they sat in the corner by themselves, talking and laughing.

"I think my parents are still up," he said as they drove home after the dance. He had driven past his house many times, but never taken her upstairs to meet any of his family.

Sandy felt this was what he intended to do tonight. "I can't wait until this summer." Sandy opened the side window. The warm April breeze, smelling of new flowers and freshly mowed lawns, filled up the car and Sandy lay back, with her head resting on the back of the seat.

"What are you going to do?"

"My parents are going to the shore. I'll probably get a job down there, work as a sales clerk in one of the department stores."

"Get some bread for college?"

She nodded her head, yes. She looked at him hopefully. "Would you come down the shore to see me? We could go swimming."

He shook his head. "I don't swim. I hate the beach. I never quite got used to taking my leg off. I did it once, when I was at the rehab center. I went with another amputee. We put our legs under a blanket, you know, wrapped them so they wouldn't get full of sand. Then we both fell asleep." Skip laughed, remembering. "Would you believe, when we woke up, our stumps were so sunburned, we couldn't put our legs back on? We made quite a sight, carrying our legs across the sand and up the steps of the boardwalk."

"It doesn't always have to be like that," Sandy said.

"But it is now," he answered. He stopped the car in front of his house. It was not like the modern split-level, rec-room, patio kind of house that Sandy was used to. But Skip's house was a strong-looking house, big, three floors high, with a front porch and a fence in back, and windows all over, the kind of windows that must have windowsills inside and radiators underneath them.

"It's a little run-down, isn't it?" Skip said. "It could use a good paint job. The fence around the back is falling apart . . . and those front steps could use a few good boards in them."

"Why don't you fix it up?" Sandy asked him. "You could paint it, Skip, and fix the steps . . . even the fence."

He shrugged. "Why bother?" he said with disinterest.

"Because you care. It's in your face when you talk about the house. That's why you brought me here. You really care, Skip."

She wouldn't meet his parents tonight. She could tell by the change in his face. He started the motor.

"Come on," she said. "Let's finish this one. This one time, let's talk it out."

He shook his head. "Nothing more to say. I don't care about anything." He looked straight at her, and deliberately added, "Or anybody."

She sat back as though she had been slapped in the face.

They passed light after light, home after home, hill after hill, without a word or a touch between them. Usually the rides in the car with Skip had seemed to go too fast. Tonight it was unbearable.

He drove up into her driveway. The light was on in front of the carport.

He started to get out.

"Don't bother," she stopped him. "Don't walk me to the door. Why bother?" She used his words.

"Okay." He looked straight ahead. "Whatever you say." How could he turn himself off so quickly, so completely?

"You told me once you weren't afraid to go to Vietnam. Remember?"

"Yes," he said quietly. "I remember."

"You said you weren't afraid of anything, getting hurt on the basketball court, splitting your head open against one of those gymnasium walls."

"I know, I said it. That's right."

"Well, now I know what you're afraid of." She turned toward him, and her eyes challenged him. "You're afraid to care, Skip, you're just scared to death to care."

She slammed the car door in his face and, without looking back, ran into the house.

• • • CHAPTER 12

"I can't stay here any more." Bennie shook his head stubbornly. "Man, I can't hang on to your coattails forever."

Glen sat with the plays for the basketball game in front of him. "Bennie, you're not going to sleep in a car. Things will break for you soon. So be patient. Come on, go over this stuff with me."

Bennie sighed. "They're a tough team," he cautioned.

"The champions, no less, for three years. There's

no way to outshoot them. That's why I think some stall basketball is the best."

"It looked good at practice last night. I just wish Skip had been there." Bennie looked worried. "He didn't sound good on the phone. But he wouldn't talk so I didn't pry. I just hope he gets there tonight."

"He's never let us down yet," Glen said. "Now look," he pointed to the sketches, "just keep that figure eight going, and keep moving on the court. As long as no one comes toward you, you can keep that ball as long as you want. Sit there and tie your shoelaces. Wait for the lay-up and then, only then, shoot."

"I hope the other guys keep their cool." Bennie shook his head. "Stall ball is a controlled game. They're not going to like it."

"Like it or not. We're going to keep those champions from scoring. They haven't scored less than fifty points all season."

Glen picked up his jacket. "I'm going over to the gym early. I want to set up the chairs, and those nets look bad. One of the kids is going to help put new ones on."

"I wish the gym was better." Bennie wheeled with him to the door.

Glen shrugged. "We have no place else. The Shady Hollow gym was booked. This place is much smaller. There's going to be a lot of crack-ups against those walls. We'll just caution the spectators to keep their toes in." Glen slung the knapsack of basketballs over his shoulder, tucked the plans in his pocket, and waved as he closed the door behind him.

The radio on the desk came alive. It was Black Diamond. They had had several long conversations this week. Bennie was getting closer. But Diamond's 73s always came when Bennie got too close.

"How do you really feel about that?" Bennie'd ask. "About being alone?"

"73s."

Or, "Man, get out here with the rest of us."

"73s."

Bennie sighed. Walls, walls, walls. Why did people have to build them? They took so long to put up, and so long to knock down. He answered Black Diamond. "Good evening, America."

"You're feeling good."

"Big game tonight."

"Who with?"

"The Eastern Jets."

"They're the ones you said had won the championship last year."

"Yup."

"You don't stand a chance. That's what you said," Black Diamond insisted.

"That's right. But we're sure going to give it a try."

"What for?" Black Diamond's voice goaded him on. "You know you're going to lose."

"But maybe we can shake them up. Man, that's a moral victory."

"You can't win a championship on a moral victory."

"But it's one to keep in your pocket for life."

Silence. Then, "I'd rather win, or not play."

Bennie laughed. "If you don't play, how you know you're not going to win?"

"Some things are sure things."

"Is that your bag . . . a sure thing?"

"At least I know where I stand."

"Safe is suffocating. Safe is stagnant. Water gets polluted if it doesn't move . . . same with people."

"You think I'm polluted." Black Diamond's voice was angry.

"I think you need to move upstream."

"You don't give up," Black Diamond quipped.

"Come to the game tonight."

"Don't joke."

"I'm not laughing. It's at the Elm Street gym. Eight o'clock. Come watch us give the champions a run for their money."

"A moral victory?"

"It could work both ways. I'll pick you up."

"Nope. If I get there, I'll find a ride."

"Does that mean yes?"

"That means maybe."

"I've got to get going. We want to go over some plays before the game."

"Good luck."

"Come say it in person."

"73s."

Do I have you, Black Diamond, or are you going to float by me each time? Bennie wondered as he changed into his uniform. He pulled up his long white stretch socks, put on the green uniform, zipped up the jacket. He glanced quickly at the clock on the top of the kitchen counter. Seven o'clock. Fifteen minutes to get to the gym. That would give him a half hour to warm up. Stall ball. He wondered if it would work. How do you stop a bulldozer? The champions were comparable to that.

The gym was beginning to fill up by the time he got

there. Spectators lined the walls, some standing, some crouched in corners, others just sitting on the floor. The Jets were warming up already, in the far end of the court.

Bennie began to unzip his jacket. "Hey." Mac slapped his hand as he wheeled by, then shot one into the basket. "We're shooting good."

Bennie laughed. "Psyche it up," he said.

"Bennie!" Sandy called out his name and ran over. Carrie and Buddy wheeled behind her. Her face was strained. "Skip isn't here."

"So. You know that guy. Always late."

"No, you don't understand. He didn't get his leg back in time." Sandy put up her hands, as though helpless.

"It was supposed to be ready yesterday."

"I know that, Bennie. But it was something about a part. I don't know exactly, but he's without his leg."

"Did he call you?"

"No." She reddened. "He called Mac."

"He won't show up without that leg." Buddy shook his head.

"I know." Sandy kneeled down beside Bennie's chair. "None of us have ever seen him without it. Bennie, without him here tonight, you won't stand a chance."

Bennie didn't have to be told that. He knew it already. Skip's anger, his head-on collisions, his gutsy opposition was what the team counted on to shake up the opposition. Skip was the man they watched and feared—stall game or no stall game, he had to be here.

"Bennie, do you know where he lives?" Buddy asked.

Bennie nodded yes.

"What do you think?" Bennie looked at Buddy.

"Let's try," Bud said at last.

"We have to try," Carrie's voice shook. "We just can't forget about him."

The four of them left the gym quickly. "How much time do we have?" Bennie asked.

"One half hour." Buddy looked at his watch.

Skip's house was just a five-minute ride from the Elm Street gym.

"Right there." Sandy pointed. "The end house."

The bottom part of the house was dark. Two small lights shone from the windows upstairs.

Carrie looked up at the winding steps to the porch. "That takes care of us," she said.

Sandy turned around, frightened.

"Aren't you coming with me?"

Bennie turned to her. "Sandy, there's no way, woman, to get us up those steps! It's up to you now."

Sandy looked at the steps. Trapped. She hadn't thought about them. All the time they were driving to Skip's house, she had been thankful that she wouldn't have to face him alone, face him when he looked at her knowing she saw him differently, face his anger, his hurt. At least she could lean on Bennie's soft gentle voice, on Buddy's sense of humor, on the fact that Skip wouldn't want to make a scene in front of Carrie. But she had been undone by fifteen old, tired, wooden steps.

"I don't know if I can." She hesitated.

"Well, then, get up there and see if you can," Bennie's voice was impatient. "Time is running out."

She got out of the car and left them sitting there, feeling their eyes follow her up the steps.

She knocked on the front door.

The door opened. Skip stood there on crutches, his pants leg tied into a knot where the wooden leg would have been. His face turned pale with shock when he saw her.

He tried to shut the door, but she was caught halfway in between so he let it swing open and turned his back on her.

For a moment he looked defenseless. She had become so used to his standing on two feet, whether his or not, that she was unprepared for her own reaction. She went to touch his shoulder but he pulled away. He threw the crutches to the floor, hopped over to a chair and sat down. Then for the first time their eyes met. There was the anger, the coldness she had grown so used to seeing. The shades of Skip's soul were pulled down tight again. He hadn't changed. With or without the leg, his eyes told her that.

She walked over to him, wanting to speak, but his eyes stopped her. The crutches lay between them. So much was inside her, so much to say. "Skip . . . don't close me out."

She bent down to pick up the crutches. His good foot came down on her hand, not harshly, yet not gently. It just sat on her hand, stopping her right where she was. She knelt there for a moment, her hand trapped between the crutches and his foot, her long hair sweeping into her mouth and about her eyes. She didn't move. The future hung between them, fragile, perishable, as the seconds passing by begged for an answer.

Tears spilled down Sandy's cheeks. She couldn't keep them from coming. With her free hand, she tried to wipe them away. But then she just gave up, kneeling before him, the sobs coming from deep within her. She looked up at him at last, with everything she had to say in her eyes . . . on her tear-stained face.

He lifted her gently from the floor and held her for a moment midway between the floor and the chair. "I'm not worth it," he said and the storm left his eyes. "You know that."

"I think you are," she said softly.

He let her go and sat back in the chair for a long moment, just looking at her. She let him look, watching his face grow warm and then a smile etch his lips. He bent down and grabbed the crutches.

They walked out of the apartment silently.

Three eager faces greeted them from the car. They reached the gym five minutes before game time. Glen was going out of his mind. "Where were you?" he called to them when they wheeled in. "Never mind, don't answer me. Skip, it's stall ball. Figure eight. Keep your eyes on Bennie. Get into your uniforms. If you guys ever pull anything like this on me again! . . ."

Sandy took Glen over to the side and explained what had happened while Buddy and Skip went into the locker room. They would never forget that game, the audience, the Eastern Jets, or the Zippers. The Zippers kept the ball tucked inside them like a golden egg, only losing it now and then, only shooting when the shot was perfect. The Jets didn't know what was happening. They kept racing to the opposite end of the court, waiting for that play that didn't come while the Zippers casually formed the moving circle eight, playing the ball back and forth, constantly moving, unnerving and shaking up the champions until they fumbled, fouled, and even missed the baskets in their frustration.

It was like watching a ballet, the perfect timing of the moving wheels, the control. Even Skip, who preferred to play a heavy, almost wild, defense, kept his cool, holding on to the ball, passing it to Bennie, back to Buddy then Mac and Jim, back and forth until the opening was there and then the beautiful sound of the ball swooshing into the basket.

The Eastern Jets couldn't be wiped out. They were too strong. Even though their shots were fewer than ever before in a game, it was enough to make a win. The game was a pure pro game and when the final score was counted, 30 to 28, even the Jets came over to them with renewed respect.

"You're a team now," they said. "You're real champions."

"Beautiful game," the refs commented and the audience stood up and cheered as the Zippers wheeled by.

"We couldn't score," said one of the Jets. "First time we've been held down."

"We're in second place." Glen came into the locker room after the game. "Not bad for a young team. Next stop is the Regionals in Ohio!" He patted each of the fellows on the shoulders, his face shining with pride. "Did you see Jim Mazer out there, right in the front row? What a show game you put on."

No one was tired. Relaxed, exhilarated even in defeat, the team experienced the taste of victory that went deeper than just a scoreboard. It had been a good game.

"Skip, you played beautiful ball." Glen handed him his crutches and Skip hopped out of the wheelchair.

"Thanks for coming." He shook Skip's hand. He knew what it had taken for Skip to come out on that court tonight. Those guts would help him through whatever it took to live without a leg.

Sandy called through the opened door. "May I come in?" Her voice was strained.

"Sure," Glen waved her in. "What's up?"

"Jim Mazer, he had to leave. His son's been hurt in an automobile accident. Oh, Glen, they said he's in critical condition."

Glen put on his jacket. "I'm going over to the hospital. Clear up the gym, fellows. See that the chairs are put away, and lock up. I'll see you later."

A pall fell over the locker room. Many of them knew about automobile accidents, about nearly dying.

Bennie rolled out of the locker room slowly. A deep sadness welled inside him. He could almost hear the wail of ambulance sirens, the hush at the hospital. He was so deep in his own thoughts that he didn't hear the voice next to him until it repeated itself. "Blue?"

Bennie looked up. What he saw was beautiful. He saw a young man in a wheelchair. His hands were gloved, lying crossed in his lap. A black beard veiled his chin.

He slowly lifted a gloved hand and with extreme care, placed it in Bennie's. It was a beautiful hand, though slightly bent and with limited response, but still a most beautiful hand. It was Black Diamond's.

··· CHAPTER 13

Carrie sat on her bed, her lips pursed, her blue eyes
worried, unsure. Was she doing the right thing? Even
now, so close to leaving, she wasn't sure.

Her suitcase was packed. It contained her clothes for
the weekend. She had been sure of everything for so long
that uncertainty hung like an unfamiliar robe around her.
When she had first been taken ill with polio, she knew
she would never walk again. That she had been sure of.
Her parents had adjusted the house to her needs so that
she could reach everything and get around with a great
deal of comfort.

She had that all around her, comfort and safety and certainty. They would always take care of her, and when her parents could no longer be with her, they had made provisions that someone would always tend to her needs. Those were the certainties.

She looked around her room, at the drapes, pink and purple, she had sewed herself. The bedspread to match lay under the stuffed animals that sat staring back at her.

"Come over on Friday night for dinner and stay for the weekend," Ina had coaxed.

It had seemed such a casual invitation, but both Ina and Carrie knew how much weighed on it. Ina wanted Carrie to move in with her, to share the apartment. She felt Carrie could do some sewing and hemming to pay her expenses and, when able, to take some courses at the rehab center near by.

"Secretarial work," Ina had suggested. "Or tailoring, maybe."

Carrie had listened to Ina map out the wonder of it all. It was such a perfect apartment, big enough for two wheelchairs to get easily around in. It was just about an hour away from her own home.

Last night she had told her parents at supper. Sandy had promised to help her break it to them.

"I'm staying at Ina's this weekend," she had said.

Her mother stopped chewing and put down her fork.

Her father wiped his mouth with the napkin. "Those Zippers. They've really taken over," he commented.

Sandy smiled. "They're great. I wish you'd get to know them better."

"It's difficult to get to know them at all. They're always on the move."

Carrie laughed. "They do get around. But that's because they're involved in so much."

"You've never been away from home before, Carrie. What is Ina like?"

Carrie remembered the conversation as she straightened the bedspread. Sandy had chimed in, "Ina's great. You'd love her, Mom. She works in a nursing home for crippled children. She's the receptionist."

"Where's her family?" her father had asked.

"In Chicago."

Sandy's mother had looked over at her father and her eyebrows went up a half degree. "Why would she move so far from her family. Didn't they want her?"

Carrie got the message. "Mom, you don't move away from home just because your parents don't want you."

"If you have a good home," her father had countered, "why would you move?"

She had wheeled away from the table last night, disappointed that they couldn't share what was probably the most important weekend of her life. Such a simple thing for someone else. For her, a giant step. And they couldn't share it. The wonder. The excitement. The fear.

Well, I'm going. I'm really going. Her thoughts came back to the present. She looked out the window, searching for Ina's car.

"All of a sudden, you don't like this house," her father had said accusingly just before she had gone to bed.

"Ina's different from you," her mother had pleaded

before she turned off Carrie's lights. "You don't really know what the outside world is all about. It's cruel, Carrie, and you're so sensitive. We would have seen to it that you would never be hurt."

Carrie thought about being hurt. Hurt was days spent hemming and stitching, adjusting dresses for women who had to be somewhere that Saturday. Carrie had seen the excitement in their eyes when they spoke of their fabulous weekends or dinner dances or cruises. She would stitch up the hems silently and wonder.

Her aunts and uncles would come over with their children, often in the late afternoon for visits, perhaps some to stay for dinner, and her parents would carry out the bowls of spaghetti and ravioli, and food would spread across the table like a blanket of comfort. It was good. It was warm. It was safe. So why didn't she just stick to it?

She rolled over to the closet and pulled out a box tied up neatly. The box bulged with chest pulleys and dumbbells, the equipment Glen had given her to build up her arms for swimming and archery.

The Zippers had changed her. This house was safe but it wasn't living . . . not for her. She was part of other people's lives here. But what of her own? Maybe some day her parents would understand.

The horn beeped outside.

"Ina's here," Carrie's mother called.

Carrie wheeled out of her bedroom, her valise on her lap.

"Here, I'll help you," her mother offered but Carrie waved her off. "It's okay, Mom. I can manage." Mrs. Dennis bent over and kissed her.

"The phone number's on the dining room table," Carrie told her.

"I'll call you," she said.

"I'm coming, Ina." Carrie pushed open the front door and wheeled down the driveway.

"Are you coming to stay?" Ina joked. "What a suitcase." She lifted the suitcase, as her arms were much stronger than Carrie's, and tossed it in the back seat. Carrie slid into the seat next to her, folded up her wheelchair and stacked it in the back seat.

"Ready?" Ina looked at her. "Was it bad?"

Carrie's eyes filled with tears. Only Ina would have understood and asked that question. She shook her head yes.

Ina started the car. "Dry your tears, Carrie. We've got a busy weekend coming up."

Carrie was exhausted by the time she got everything unpacked in Ina's apartment. The excitement, the strange surroundings, the phone calls from members of the team. "Hey, Carrie, congratulations on coming out." They joked with her and made her feel at ease until the strained events of the night before with her parents faded.

Some of the Zippers even came over to visit later that night. It was three in the morning before Carrie finally fell wearily into bed. She looked up at the ceiling. There were no flowers like the ones she had counted for so many years on the ceiling of her room. She was too sleepy even to count. She just rolled over in the bed contentedly.

"Homesick?" Ina asked before she fell asleep.

"Not yet," came the answer.

Saturday was a day that none of the Zippers was really looking forward to. Glen had arranged a benefit game for Jim Mazer's son. The boy was paralyzed from the chin down, being fed intravenously, almost a vegetable. Glen had been visiting him all week, trying to keep Jim's spirits up. He was familiar, so familiar, with the plight of the paralyzed and those affected around him.

Glen had told Carrie that Jim's son, Bob, was beginning to move his eyes in answer to questions from his family. Standing there next to Jim, Glen had thought of the benefit. He knew Jim didn't need the money, but that he needed to know people cared. So the Zippers had agreed to put on a game in honor of Bob Mazer and his struggle to live.

Carrie sat on the edge of the bed, just waking up. She smelled bacon, and the aroma of coffee, freshly perked, floated through the doorway. It was only eight o'clock. She was never up that early at home.

"Get up, lazybones. Breakfast. We have a busy day," Ina called from the kitchen.

Carrie amazed herself at breakfast. She ate everything and doubled the usual portions.

"For a small one, you sure can put it away." Ina poured her a second cup of coffee.

Carrie laughed. "I don't eat like this usually." But the excitement of not knowing what the day would hold had given her an appetite.

"Hey, I'll clear off the table, and you can take a bath and get ready." Ina put some of the dishes in her lap. "We'll take shifts. The game's at noon so that'll give us plenty of time."

"Fine." Carrie left the table. "But can't I help just a little?" she offered.

"You'll take care of the dinner shift, okay? Let's see what kind of miracle you can cook up then."

Carrie got her things together in the bedroom and started toward the bathroom. Suddenly she stopped.

Ina was behind her. She opened up the linen closet. "Here are all the towels you'll need." Then, noticing Carrie's indecision, she asked her, "What is it Carrie?"

"You're not going to believe this," Carrie confided, ashamed even to say it, "but I've never taken a bath by myself. I mean, I don't even know how to get in the tub without breaking my neck." She didn't look at Ina. If she laughed at her, she might die right there.

Ina's hand was on her shoulder. "Okay, Carrie. We all went through it. We all had to learn how to get into a tub."

"You too?" Carrie's eyes filled with tears.

"Me too," Ina smiled. "So today, Carrie, you shall learn to take a bath. By that I mean," Ina said slowly and jokingly, "you shall get into the tub and out of the tub by yourself. Now you go in and get ready. Fill up the tub while you're in the wheelchair."

Carrie filled up the tub. Then she got undressed. Her heart was pounding, almost throbbing in her chest, and her whole body trembled. "You nut," she said to herself over and over again, "who in this world should be afraid to get into a tub?" But she was. She knew it and Ina knew it, too.

"Okay. Ready?" came the voice from behind the closed door.

"Okay," Carrie answered and took a deep breath.

"Turn your chair and face the tub. Now swing your foot-peddles away from in front of the chair and place your legs over the rim of the tub while you're still sitting in the wheelchair. Got it?"

"They're over." Carrie felt her feet dangling in the warm water. It was almost like being in the pool. She remembered sitting at the edge of the pool, her feet dipping into the water, before she slid in.

"Now let yourself slide onto the rim of the tub. Hold on to your wheelchair for support and hold on to the rim of the tub. Be careful."

Carrie slid slowly. One hand was on the rim, the other on the wheelchair. "I'm going to fall," she called out. "I can't. . . ."

"Oh no you're not." Ina's voice was strong. "You wouldn't dare drown in my apartment."

Carrie steadied herself on the rim. "Okay," she exclaimed breathlessly, "I'm here."

"Good." Ina's voice was relieved. "Now let yourself slide slowly into the tub."

The splash of water wet Carrie as her body slid into the tub. It had taken her about twenty minutes of maneuvering, but she had made it. She had done it by herself at last.

Ina sat on the other side of the door waiting. All she heard was a splash. She held her breath, ready to open the door if necessary, and then she smiled as Carrie's voice came up through the doorknob singing, "Oh, what a beautiful morning."

The phone rang. "Call me if you need me," Ina called out and wheeled over to the phone.

"Hello, Ina?"

"Yes?"

"This is Mrs. Dennis."

"Oh, hi Mrs. Dennis."

"Can I speak to Carrie?"

"She's in the tub right now."

Silence. "By herself?" Shocked disbelief.

Ina laughed. "She likes her privacy."

Panic now. "But she could get hurt. How did she get in?"

"By herself. She managed very well."

"But . . . how will she get out? You must help her out."

"She'll get out the same way she got in," Ina answered. "Look, Mrs. Dennis, she's really okay. I'll have her call you when she gets out."

"Ina, please, this is no joking matter. That child. . . ."

"She's not a child, Mrs. Dennis," Ina interrupted, "she's a young woman, and young women should be able to take their own baths."

The voice grew chilly at the other end. "Please have her call."

"Will do," Ina answered.

She put down the phone. "Mrs. Dennis, you are going to suffer, while Carrie grows," she mumbled to herself. She felt sorry for the woman. She wasn't ready for the world that Carrie was reaching out for. It was going to be a tug-of-war.

"I'm ready," came Carrie's voice from the tub.

"Okay." Ina was on the other side of the door again. "Put one of those towels on your wheelchair so that when you sit down, you don't drench your chair. Leave the water in the tub. It'll give you buoyancy getting out of it. Now back up, using your hands to pull yourself back up on the rim."

"Oh, boy," Carrie's quivering voice came from inside the tub. "This is tough."

"How you doin'? It's tricky. Oh yeah, put a small towel on the rim so you don't slip."

"I'm on the rim."

"Is your wheelchair steady?"

"It's braced against the wall."

"Good. Grab hold of it with one hand and push against the rim with the other. You should land on target."

"I'm in the wheelchair. I did it!" Carrie's jubilant voice came from the bathroom. "How long did it take me?"

"About an hour altogether. Not bad for the first time. I hope you do better at the Nationals."

Carrie laughed. "Ina, you're nuts."

Carrie returned the call to her mother. She finally convinced her that she had survived the bath without bruises or injury to herself. It quieted her mother temporarily. Carrie and Ina had a quick lunch, then hurried to the game. There were at least a thousand people in the stands, friends and followers of Jim Mazer, all there to pay honor to Bob and the courageous battle he was fighting.

The Zippers played once again against the Eastern Jets and both teams played with all their heart. Bennie scored time after time. Buddy tried hard for the outside shots giving the audience one thrill after another, and Skip, playing with his leg on this time, was a human dynamo, many times crashing against the walls because

of his unbelievable speed. All the members of both basketball teams were thinking of Bob while they played on
that court. They knew the feeling of long months in the
hospital, lying on one's back between life and death, not
feeling anything from the neck or waist or the legs. They
knew what it was like to be cut off from the outside, while
nerve ends died and life hung precariously between de-
spondency and hope.

Jim Mazer's face showed his suffering. His eyes had
dark rings around them and as he sat in the front row,
his hands clenched, then unclenched.

Toward the first half of the game, Bennie noticed he
had gone.

"What happened?" he asked Buddy. "Why did he
leave?"

"Don't know." Buddy looked over the crowd again.
"But it doesn't look good."

The end of the game left them exhausted. Sweat
dripped off their backs, and biceps flexed as the Zippers
heard the horn blow at the end of the game.

And then Glen was walking onto the center of the
court. The team grew hushed, the audience still, as if a
flutter of premonition filled the room, and only the tick
of the loud clock at the top of the gymnasium wall broke
the silence.

"Ladies and gentlemen," Glen's voice broke. He
stopped for a second, then looked at the Zippers, then
over to the crowd. "Bob Mazer died a short while ago."

A gasp, a slow-traveling moan swept across the
stands. Then silence.

Skip stood there stunned. He hadn't known Bob but
he had thought he knew what it was like to feel it was all

over. Something in him had responded to that boy's battle for life. But he was dead now . . . gone.

Skip huddled against the wall, deep in the shadows, and for the first time since his leg had been blown into pieces, deep uncontrollable sobs racked his body. He was crying for Bob. He was crying, because suddenly, he was glad just to be alive.

· · · **CHAPTER 14**

"You'll have your dream, Glen. You'll have the center."
It was Jim Mazer's voice at the other end of the phone,
just a week after his son's funeral.

"Jim." Glen groped for words. "What can I say?"

"It'll be called the Bob Mazer Memorial. Come over
to my office next week."

The telephone clicked and Glen just stood there,
holding the phone until Bennie picked the receiver from
his hand and placed it on the cradle.

The next week brought with it many changes. The
basketball season was over and track and field practice

began in earnest. The warm May weather was just perfect for practicing in the park adjoining the Shady Hollow High School. Javelin and discus throwing, weight lifting, the dashes, filled the park with onlookers as the Zippers began the big changeover from the basketball season to getting ready for the National competition.

Glen tried not to think about Jim Mazer or his son or the center. His feelings were mixed ones of anticipation and sadness. He didn't look forward to seeing Jim. The last time they had spoken, Jim had just left the room where his son had died. The look on his face, such sudden grief, had turned Glen's face to the hospital wall.

Carrie called him during the week. "Glen, can you come over?" She was crying. "I'm ready to make the move. I'm going to move in with Ina. Things are terrible here because of it. Can you come over?"

"Tonight . . . about eight."

"Want to come?" Glen asked Bennie later. "I can use some support."

Bennie shook his head and waved him off. "No thanks. I'll pass this one by. Besides, I just might drop by to see Black Diamond tonight. There are a few apartments we might take a look at."

"So long then. Wish me luck." Glen put on his team jacket. "I always feel better wearing it," he said.

Carrie's house was lit up when he got there. The light on the front door was bright and warm. He wondered what the reception would be inside.

Sandy answered the door.

"Hey, it's Glen. I thought you were Skip," Sandy confided. "He said he was coming over tonight."

Carrie wheeled into the living room. Sandy left them alone.

"What made you decide to leave?" Glen sat down on the chair next to Carrie, his cap folded in between his hands.

"I've got to try it." She twisted her graceful fingers nervously. "I can get some odd jobs sewing. That should help pay my way. And if the rehab center will take me, I'll go there for a year and learn secretarial work. I've just got to try."

Glen looked around the room. It was a comfortable room, one that Carrie must have spent many hours in . . . happy hours, hours she might have forgotten about. She was trying for a different type of happiness now.

"It's not going to be easy," he cautioned her. "You're going to have to go out scratching for a dollar. You've never really known what it's like to make your own way."

Carrie nodded. "I know," she said. "But whatever I do earn, I'll be helping toward Ina's rent. She's paying it all now. I can certainly earn enough for my food and small expenses. I'm earning that now. And then around Christmas time, you know I always make those Christmas stockings. That brings in some money."

Her parents came into the room.

Glen stood up. "Carrie called me over," he explained.

They sat down in silence. Mr. Dennis cleared his throat. "We don't want her to leave."

Mrs. Dennis pleaded, "We'll let her do what she wants, but please, help us to convince her she must do it from here."

"Everything was all right here, until the Zippers came along." Mr. Dennis looked accusingly at Glen.

"What right do you have to meddle in other people's lives . . . to change their lives so abruptly?"

"Daddy . . . Mother . . . please." Carrie was visibly upset.

"It's okay, Carrie," Glen said softly. "I don't think it's really up to you or me, Mr. Dennis. We just showed Carrie what she was capable of doing, perhaps even how she might find a way to live her own life. The rest is up to her. If she thinks she can handle it, who's to say she can't? Why not give her the chance to try?"

"We don't think she can," Mr. Dennis insisted.

"I'm going anyway." Carrie's voice was quiet. Mrs. Dennis looked over at her and saw the unmoving determination in her eyes. She ran from the room crying.

"We're upset right now. Will you excuse us?" Mr. Dennis left the room.

Glen looked over at Carrie. "It's tough to say good-bye," he said, "even under the best of terms."

She wheeled over to him. "If it's so hard, why do I feel I still have to try?"

He took her hand in his. "Try, Carrie," he said. "They'll come around. And eventually they'll find themselves on your side. They're actually on your side right now. They're just scared."

He left her sitting alone in the living room, alone to fight the most important battle of her life. He wasn't sure if she'd make it. It was one thing to say you're going to move, another to do it, to pack the bag, give away the things you can't take with you, say good-bye to the familiar bed and couch and walls, and tree in the backyard, tuck away the memories, and try for something new. She was still on the other side of the door, in the house. He had to leave her alone, to find her own way out. Whether she was tough enough to do it, he didn't know.

The meeting with Jim Mazer took place the following day. Glen took Bennie who took his guitar on the back of his chair.

"Must we?" Glen asked, pointing to the guitar.

"Just for luck." Bennie plucked two notes in answer.

The meeting was a different one than last time. There seemed to be no decision at all to make. Jim Mazer, haggard, now a shell of the man he was, sat at the head of the table with the plans before him.

"It's going to be the best center this country has ever seen," he said softly.

For Bob, Glen thought, and all the Bobs who didn't make it.

"I want every conceivable program, for paras and quads, in that center."

"We'll have to watch out for ease of circulation and the graphics have to be great," Glen cautioned.

"There's an architect who has already agreed to start work on it." Jim Mazer stood up and walked toward the bay window behind his desk. "There's a piece of land, right outside Shady Hollow. I own it," he offered. "I thought some day Bob . . . well." He sat down again, his feet almost giving way from under him. "That's where the center will be."

"The money?" Glen had to know.

"It has been appropriated, and I'll keep it coming in. I have many friends who are interested. They'll back me up."

Bennie tapped his guitar lightly. Softly, so no one could hear, he hummed to the beat coming from beneath his fingers and moved his head to the rhythm.

Glen and Bennie sat there the rest of the afternoon, passing on suggestions, offering new ones, drawing Jim into it whenever they could. Glen's heart ached for the man. That the center should be built on a man's sadness seemed an irony in itself.

"I'll be clearing the land next week," Jim said at last.

"What day?" Glen asked as they were about to leave.

"Why?"

"We want to be there."

Jim smiled, his first smile since his son had died. "Wednesday morning . . . about eight-thirty."

Wednesday morning about eight-thirty they were there, as many of the Zippers who could get off from work, and their friends; a crowd that multiplied by word of mouth until about three hundred people gathered around on the land that once was to be Bob Mazer's.

The excavation trucks swept up the hill, the dump trucks and their crews breaking the morning stillness. Jim Mazer was out there too.

"Man, it's only dirt, but it's beautiful," Bennie sighed.

"Play the guitar, Bennie," Carrie coaxed. She hummed softly as Bennie's music drifted through the crowd. Next to Bennie sat Black Diamond. Sandy and Skip, Ina and Buddy were with a small group off to the side.

A tree went down and then another. The work had begun.

Bennie looked toward the wooded lot. He saw hope for another Bennie who might be looking for an apartment. He'd find his, maybe tomorrow, but another Bennie would find it easier. The center would see to that.

Carrie's eyes filled. The center would have a rehab

center, a place to learn skills, a placement bureau. Maybe by the time it was built, she'd be ready. No, not maybe. She *would* be ready.

Ina and Buddy grabbed each other's hands and clung to each other, looking over the vastness of the land. "It's going to be beautiful," Buddy exclaimed.

Jim Mazer walked across the hills alone. It was Bob's land. He would bring it to life.

Glen stood by himself, in the back where the trucks were, almost hidden by some of the thick trees. He didn't see the trucks or the crowds or hear the trees fall. He saw paras and quads wheeling in and out of the center; buses pulling up, unloading busy active people. He saw wheel-chairs go in the doors of the center, wheeled by paras unsure and uncertain, who would come out ready to face life. He heard the shouts from the basketball games and the loud cheers as the girl swimmers sped across the pool. He heard the javelin hit the ground and the Ping-Pong balls smack across the table as the people at the center learned, and played, and found themselves.

He saw the faces, hundreds of them, filing in and out through the center door. He looked up toward the sky. Somewhere up there, on top of the building, reaching out toward the highest cloud, would be the emblem of basketball and wheelchair sports . . . a man in a wheel-chair holding a torch.

He saw it all. There on the hill. On Bob's land.

The beginning.

ASSOCIATIONS
AND PUBLICATIONS
OF INTEREST
TO THE READER

The Disabled Driver's Association
The Magic Carpet Magazine
The Blue Star House
Highgate Hill
London N., England

Rehabilitation Gazette
4502 Maryland Avenue
St. Louis, Missouri   63108

National Association of Physically Handicapped
Newsletter

124 West South Boundary
Perrysburg, Ohio   43551

Achievement
North Dade Branch YMCA
13855 Northwest 17th Avenue
Miami, Florida   33054

The Canadian Paraplegic Association
The Caliper Magazine
153 Lyndhurst Avenue
Toronto, 178 Ontario, Canada

The Paraplegic News
935 Coastline Drive
Seal Beach, California   90740

Accent On Living
Gillum Road and High Drive
P.O. Box 726
Bloomington, Illinois   61701

Handy-Cap Horizon
3250 East Loretta Drive
Indianapolis, Indiana   46227

VEEP Very Exciting Employment Program
P.O. Box 181
Plymouth Meeting, Pennsylvania   19462